AF448122

Hope in the Storm

Hope in the Storm

B. J. Swanson

Copyright © 2024 by Beverly J. Swanson

All rights reserved. This book may not be reproduced or used in any manner whatsoever without the express written permission of the publisher except for the use of brief quotations in a book review or scholarly journal.

First Printing: 2024

ISBN 797-889034514-1

Lifetime Writings
P. O. Box 1205
Murrells Inlet, SC 29576

www.bevswansonbooks.com

Books by B. J. Swanson

<u>Loyalties Trilogy</u>
Misguided Loyalties
Contingent Loyalties
Betrayed Loyalties

<u>Murrells Inlet Beach Series</u>
I Believe in You
As Waves on the Sand
In the Fullness of Time
Taproom
A Rose in the Marsh
A Wink and A Prayer
Stronger Together
Hope in the Storm

From This Day Forward
A Country Music Christmas
Secrets & Lies
All That Came Before

<u>Short Story Books</u>
For Love of the Story
The Blue Tractor
Different, But the Same

Available on Amazon.com

Acknowledgements

I love living in the state of South Carolina. Although I'm not a native, I consider Murrells Inlet home. The people are gracious, considerate, positive and patriotic. I also love living near the beach, as the characters in my books do. Even though they are all fictitious and not meant to represent any actual people, they have become like friends, helping me to heal from a great loss in my life. I will always be thankful for the time they have occupied my mind.

The restaurant Taproom in Murrells Inlet is also fictitious, but the other establishments mentioned were real at the time of these writings. If you ever get to the South Strand, be sure and look them up. They will not disappoint.

With the writing of this series, I have watched my characters change and mature. I believe this is a healthy design of human nature. The Bible says God has a plan and a purpose for each of us, and the first step in the search for our purpose is getting to know God's love personally through his son Jesus. I didn't want my characters to be traditionally religious, yet finding how God fit into each life was important to me. My desire is that watching how they do life, both the good and the not-so-good behavior and attitudes, helps each of us evaluate our own lives in much the same way.

I am grateful for the encouragement and editing I have received from the educated and careful people who have helped me in the writing process. In order to not miss anyone, I will say you know who you are.

Thank you also to the many readers who have purchased my books. I appreciate all the kind words and notes telling me you have also connected to the characters. It is my joy and passion to continue finding stories and characters you will remember after you read the final page. I thank God for the gift of writing and the sense of purpose he has bestowed upon me through my books. May each one be a blessing to someone.

B. J. Swanso

Prologue

Fifteen years ago

It had been a fun evening; something I rarely experienced. Three cars of us left my cousin Kim's birthday party and met up at Waffle House. While the people I came with talked, I eavesdropped on a conversation at the table behind me by two truckers who were driving in opposite directions. As they laughed and talked about life in general terms, I wondered how much of it was true. They spoke of experiences and places that awakened in me a desire for more than my wearisome lifestyle. I'm not even sure you could call my monotonous day-to-day existence a lifestyle. When I got up to use the restroom, I was not surprised to see the man connected to the deeper voice was probably in his fifties, but the one with the Southern accent was closer to my age. He smiled at me as I walked past him.

When I came out of the restroom, the group I had arrived with was gone, the younger trucker was paying his bill to leave. I paced my steps with his, so he held the door for me as I left.

"Thank you," I smiled at him. He might have had the kindest eyes I had ever seen.

"My mama raised a gentleman," he said.

"My mama just died," I lied. "You wouldn't be heading toward Myrtle Beach, would you?" I asked, knowing from my eavesdropping that was his next stop.

"You fixing to go there?" he asked.

"I was hoping to hitch a ride from the truck stop on the interstate. My grandparents need me to help take care of them. Since my mama died, I guess I need them, too."

I'm not sure when I became such a natural at lying, but stories just naturally rolled off my tongue like melted butter on a pancake. I learned growing up that telling people what they wanted to hear made life easier. I became so proficient at it that I rarely told the truth. When you don't have friends to call out your lies, fabrications become easy.

"You're in luck," the guy with the kind eyes said. "My next stop is Myrtle Beach. I'm fixin' on getting there tomorrow afternoon after sleeping in my truck. You're welcome to ride along."

"Do you have room?" I asked, amazed at my boldness. I still lived in my parents' house and had only been out of state once in my life.

"I even have a bed," he winked, "but as I previously stated, my parents raised a gentleman."

I followed him to a large truck cab with a long trailer attached behind it.

"Do you really have a bed it there?" I asked as we approached the cab.

"I live in my truck about twenty-five days a month," he said, walking to the passenger side, and opening the high door.

I reached for the handle, and pulled myself up onto the seat. After he closed the door, I looked around. It felt the size of a small camper, but more luxurious in a way. I momentarily envied him. He got to see the world from his luxury loft above traffic, with no one criticizing his every move. His door opened, and he swung up into his private world with ease.

"Buckle up," he said, as he started the motor and we began to move away from everything I had ever known. "By the way, my name is Adam."

"I'm Sally," I lied.

"Nice to meet you Sally," he said. "My plan is to drive to my regular rest stop about two hours ahead, sleep until dawn, and then get back on the road. Is that okay with you?"

"I'm just happy for the ride," I told him.

We listened to country music as he maneuvered his big rig out of the parking lot and through intersections until we were on the interstate. It was just after midnight and traffic was light.

"I'm sorry about your mama," Adam said.

"Thanks," I replied.

"Was she sick?"

"Cancer."

"That's tough," he replied. "I expect my parents will probably go to heaven before me, but I'll hate that day. Were you and your mama close?"

"Not really," I said. "We were nothing alike. I was adopted."

"I always thought being adopted was cool," he said. "Look how many people were just born or unplanned or sometimes even unwanted, but an adopted kid was intentional. My best friend growing up was adopted. I remember the morning in Sunday School when our teacher said that originally God's people were just the Jews, but that after Jesus came, we were adopted into God's family. My friend and I smiled at each other. We knew exactly what that meant."

"You believe the stuff in the Bible is true?" I asked him.

"You don't?" he replied.

"I guess I just thought it was a bunch of stories. You know, to make people feel better or to tell the world about sin."

"Well, in a way, you're right," he said. "The answer to your question is yes. I believe everything in the Bible was written under the inspiration of God, so it is all true."

"That's a nice thing to believe," I said.

"Yes, it is," Adam smiled. "I always read a little bit from the Bible before I fall asleep. Maybe tonight I'll read out loud if you want me to."

We drove for the next two hours with Adam telling me about going to college to please his father who owned the company for which Adam drove. He said his father still held onto the hope that Adam would tire of living on the road and settle into his father's footsteps one day. When I asked if he would, he shrugged and said he'd do what he believed God wanted him to do.

"You think God wants you to drive a truck?" I asked.

"I think he gives me freedom to choose, and I like my life as it is right now. I think he'll let me know when and if he has something else for me to do."

"I never knew anyone so connected to God," I said. "I thought people who talked to God were preachers or something."

Adam laughed. "I'm no preacher," he said, "But I do get to meet interesting people like you every week."

"You think I'm interesting?" It was my turn to laugh. "This is the first time I've been out of the state I was born and raised in. There is nothing interesting about me."

"So, you are leaving everything you know to care for your grandparents in a place you have never been. I think that is a very admirable quality and takes courage to make that move," he said.

"No, it's not brave," I sighed, "It's just a decision I recently made. I really don't know where it will lead."

"You would be surprised how many people could never step out in faith like that to an unknown future."

"I'm not stepping out in faith," I said. "I don't even know if I believe in God."

"The good news is God believes in you," Adam smiled, as he reached across the cab and patted my hand.

"You don't know me," I said.

"But God does, and the Bible says he's known you since before the foundation of the earth. It also says he has a plan for your life."

"That sounds good for some people, but I'm really nothing special. I'm sure God's not interested in me. I've never once prayed a prayer to him."

"According to the Bible, he's interested in everyone he created, and he created us all. Maybe at your grandparents' house you'll find a Bible and you can read about God for yourself. You might be surprised to discover how imperfect the people in those stories are. I'm not going to preach, but I will tell you that God knew we couldn't be perfect so he sent Jesus to die so that we can have a perfect relationship with God. We can't be perfect, but Jesus was. Now tell me about your family. Did you grow up with brothers and sisters?"

I spent the next two hours creating a childhood that sounded fun and happy. Several times my stories made him laugh. By the time he pulled into the rest stop, we were both smiling. He said he was glad he picked me up.

The two comfortable seats we had been riding in were in front of what appeared to be a little room. Behind the driver's seat was a small closet, and beyond that a camper-size kitchen with an undercounter refrigerator. Above the counter was a microwave and a cabinet. Behind the passenger seat was another cabinet for storage and a small desk and swivel chair. Beyond that area was a raised bed over which hung a flat-screen TV.

After parking the truck, we walked to a large clean public restroom. When we were back in the truck, he asked if I was sleepy. He said there was a TV, but he had a long drive tomorrow and was planning on going right to sleep. I said I was tired too as I wondered about our sleeping arrangements.

Adam hung his shirt in the cabinet, so he was now wearing a white tee shirt tucked in his jeans. He kicked off his shoes, and pulled off his belt before climbing onto what appeared to be a full-size bed.

Sliding to the far wall, he patted the bed next to him and said, "Just kick off your shoes."

As promised, Adam sat in a propped-up position and read a few chapters from the Bible about finding peace and grace. He said the apostle Paul was writing to people who thought you needed to follow rules to please God, but Paul said all you needed was to believe that God sent Jesus to pay for the sins of the world. Then, he abruptly closed the Bible, set it on the shelf above the bed and said, "I'll see you in the morning."

Turning his back to me, he pushed a button that lowered the back rest, and stretched out ready to sleep. I hesitated, and then followed his example, laying down with my back to his. Once I was situated, I felt him move, but it was only to reach up and turn off the small light over our heads. The cab was still partially lit by the lights outside and a couple on the dashboard. As I realized the bed was comfortable and Adam's breathing was soft and even, I relaxed and fell asleep.

A few hours later, the mattress shifted to bring me out of a sound sleep. As an arm came around my waist, I tensed, but quickly realized Adam's breathing was still slow and even. His hand touched bare skin under the edge of my shirt as he gently pulled me to him. I wondered what I should do as I waited to see what he wanted, but nothing more happened. I realized he was still asleep. As I relaxed, I wondered who he might be dreaming about. I closed my eyes, took a deep breath and speculated on what it might be like to always feel so secure. My dreams were peaceful, mixing the idea of a God who loved me with the even breathing against my shoulder.

The mattress shifted again as Adam rolled back to facing the wall just before dawn. As sunlight began to fill the cabin, a voice behind me said, "Wake up, sleepyhead. It's time to hit the road."

I sat up and rubbed my eyes as Adam climbed around me and hit a button on the coffee maker secured to his counter. He pulled a small case from a drawer and then handed me a travel size toothpaste and a towel, throwing a second towel over his own shoulder.

"I'll meet you back here," he said, as he left the cab.

I looked at my surroundings, and realized this was his world. It had everything he needed. The night before, as he read to me, we had been sitting up against what felt like a sofa back. When he was done reading, he pushed a button and the back flattened for us to sleep. There was a computer screen on the wall above the desk, and cabinets and drawers for his two weeks' worth of clothes and needs. He had pulled a clean shirt, socks, and shorts from a drawer before exiting the cab.

I shrugged, and climbed back into the passenger seat. Taking the towel, and realizing I would have to brush my teeth with my finger, I headed toward the restroom with my bag from last night over my shoulder. At least I had a hairbrush in it. I never thought to put clean underwear in it, because I had assumed I would be going home last night. Even the party had been impromptu. I still wasn't sure why I had hitched this ride, but unbelievably it didn't feel wrong. I thought about Adam saying God had a plan for my life. I wondered if this was his plan or if he thought going to South Carolina with a stranger was as crazy as it felt.

Chapter 1
Current Day

Bella Lynn Briggs loved twilight. She sat on the balcony of her room at the Hilton Myrtle Beach Resort watching the sky change colors as the sun lowered over the city. She was a writer, an independent soul that loved the beauty of God's creation and God's people, even though her positive worldview had been challenged this past year. Sipping the sweet tea that would probably hinder her sleep, she thought about the journey that had landed her alone in a city far from home.

The following day, Bella could not believe how hot it was as she carried her last box of belongings into the condo. August along the South Carolina coast was not a great time to move. It was like a sauna outside. Luckily, she had very little to move.

Bella looked around the empty apartment to which she had unloaded her clothes and the few other possessions that fit in the Chevy Tahoe her grandfather had left to her. She lifted her travel thermos from the counter, and refilled it with ice and water from the refrigerator. Then, she boosted herself onto the kitchen island, which was the only place to sit other than the floor. Her bed was to be delivered within the hour, and her new sofa between the hours of 12:00 and 6:00. For now, that was all she needed. At some point, she would begin to make this place her own. Grandma Lettie had planned on coming with her, but she had fallen last weekend and couldn't travel, so she sent Bella on alone to this place where she knew no one. Bella was thirty-three years old, and couldn't believe her grandmother had purchased a condo for her. Granny said God told her to. Well, if God told her, then Bell figured it was okay.

Bella pushed off the island, and carried her suitcases to the bedroom walk-in closet. At least she could begin hanging clothes until her bed came. She then took the boxes marked linens, and unpacked clean towels, a shower curtain, sheets, and her western blanket. By the time her bed arrived, those boxes were empty and her bathroom was set up, complete with soft brown rugs and a framed photo of her horse over the toilet.

"Sorry, Champ," she said with a smile. "It's not the most distinguished place to hang you, but it will make me smile first thing every morning," she added, caressing the frame as her doorbell rang.

An hour later, Bella was propped up on her newly-made bed with her cell phone. She texted her grandmother that she had arrived safely, and sent her a picture of the bathroom. Until her sofa arrived, she would spend time online locating a grocery store and seeing what else was nearby. By tomorrow, she would be ready to explore what had become her new home.

The next afternoon, dressed in a white shirt with rolled up sleeves tucked into low-riding jeans and flip-flops, Bella locked her condo door to explore and shop. As she struggled with the key, a young woman exited the next-door condo with a porch that matched her own.

"Hi," she smiled to the friendly face, "I'm not sure if it's me or the lock, but I had trouble with it last night, too. My name is Bella; I just moved in."

"I'm Reba," her neighbor said. "I got home late last night, but I saw a light in your place. Are you renting for the summer?"

"No," Bella told her, "I just moved here from Colorado."

"You're a long way from home," Reba said. "Do you know anyone here?"

"Not a soul," Bella smiled.

"I did the same thing last summer," Reba told her."

"You moved here alone not knowing anybody?" Bella asked.

"Yep," Reba told her, "I came from Nashville and rented the condo online. I told Chip that I was coming for a month and then it was two and now it's been nearly a year."

"Chip?" she asked.

"He owns the condo. I'm still renting."

"Not sure if you're staying?" Bella smiled.

"Something like that," Reba said. "What made you pick Murrells Inlet?"

"It sounds crazy," Bella told her, "But my grandmother believed I should be here. The condo was her idea."

"What do you do?" Reba asked.

"That's an interesting question," Bella smiled. "I finished college and lived on a ranch. Now, it seems I'm here to write a novel, according to my grandmother."

"No way," Reba smiled, "I came for the same reason."

"To write a book? How is it going?"

"It's a complicated story, but I finished it," Reba smiled.

"I'd like to hear more," Bella said.

"I have an appointment now," Reba said, "but we'll have to get together and compare our journeys."

"I'd like that," Bella said.

"Me, too," Reba said, as they both heard the click of Bella's door lock.

"My first goal is to find groceries," Bella said, as the two walked toward the parking lot.

Reba gave her opinions on the local shops as they walked. As Bella watched Reba drive away, she wondered if she had already found a friend. It felt like they might be kindred spirits. "Thank you, God," she said as she backed out of her parking space to see what the South Strand had to offer.

Chapter 2

Later that afternoon, Bella had just opened a novel she purchased at Litchfield Books near Fresh Market when there was a knock on her door. She opened the door to Reba.

"Am I interrupting anything?" Reba asked.

"I was about to start a new book," Bella told her.

"Reading one or writing one?" Reba asked.

Bella laughed. "I'm only reading. I thought it might stimulate my mind to find a story of my own."

"I know that feeling," Reba said, holding up two small bottles of flavored water. "Want company?"

"I'd love company," Bella said. "What are these?"

"I buy them at Fresh Market," she said, as she entered the condo. "They add a little flavor to my goal to stay hydrated."

Reba handed one to Bella as she entered the condo. "I was never in here with the last owner," she commented.

"So far, I only have a sofa and a bed," Bella said. "I still have a lot to purchase. Amazon delivered the air-fryer and some fun glasses I picked out online. I figured with paper plates it was enough to get me started. Is your condo just like mine?"

"Chip remodeled everything before I rented it," she said. "It's pretty cool and I rented it furnished. It came with everything including a Barney sofa."

"A Barney sofa?" Bella asked.

"That's what Chip called it. It's purple," Reba said, "The color of Barney, but it is actually pretty cool. He inherited the condo from his grandparents and redid the whole place before marrying a woman who owned a house on the marsh. They chose to live there and rent the condo."

"Another grandmother story," Bella commented. "How did you end up here?   Did you have a grandparent or parent influencing your life, too?"

"You could say that," Reba said, as she sat on Bella's mocha colored leather sofa. "My grandfather who I adored nudged me to take chances. When he died last year, he left me the money to take a sabbatical from my research job to try my hand at writing. My parents influenced me in a different way. I wanted to be nothing like them."

"Are they still living?" Bella asked.

"They are retired in Indiana," Reba said. "They showed up when I first moved here, but they didn't stay. What about your parents?"

"They were both killed when I was a kid. I lived in Mexico until my Grandma Lettie decided I should live with her and go to an American school. After they died, I stayed on the ranch with my grandparents."

"Did you like living on a ranch?" Reba asked.

"Yes. I loved it, and always assumed I'd stay there," Bella said.

"So, why are you here?"

"My grandmother is not one to argue with," Bella told her, "Especially when she claims God told her something."

"One of those," Reba said, "My parents were all about God and rules, too."

"My grandmother listened to God, but she wasn't big on rules," Bella said

"I'm not sure I know what that means," Reba said.

"I'm still figuring it out," Bella smiled.

"So, you just moved because your grandmother told you?" Reba asked.

"If you knew my grandmother, that's what you do," Bella laughed.

"I have helicopter parents that wanted to run my life, but I always resented it," Reba told her.

"It's not like she bosses me around," Bella said, "She doesn't make decisions without consulting God, so I trust her."

"Are you going to write books about God?"

"I don't think so," she laughed. "I'd like to write stories about people who have to overcome obstacles in their life."

"Religious stories?" Reba asked.

"Heavens no," Bella laughed, "My grandma loves Jesus, but she hates religion. She said one is all about rules and behavior; the other is only about loving God and loving people."

"I guess my parents were both," Reba said.

"According to Grandma Lettie, that's impossible. You either worship God or you worship yourself."

"I'm not sure I understand," Reba said.

Bella laughed. "Maybe someday you'll meet my grandma. She gave me Grandpa's car, and was supposed to come with me until she fell. I'm sure she'll visit when she's able. I don't have much food in the house. Should we go find something to eat that someone else cooks and serves us?"

"I know just where we should go. Chip owns a restaurant called Taproom," Reba said. "I'll drive."

As the two of them drove to Taproom, Reba listened to Bella talk. With her thick, dark hair and dark brown eyes, she was beautiful, but her most striking feature was her laugh. There was an infectious quality in her laidback attitude that would make people assume her life had been pampered and carefree, but Reba doubted that had been the case. Someday, Reba would ask how her parents had died.

Chapter 3

Sandy Asher hummed as she finished cleaning up her kitchen. Wiping the counter one more time, she stopped to look out at the ocean view of which she never tired. Today was her fourth wedding anniversary, and she reflected, her fourth time to celebrate such an occasion. Her first time had been with Donny. They were just kids and deliriously happy to be pregnant. Donny had died in a ski accident before Mitch was born. She still smiled when she remembered that immature and carefree relationship. Then out of loneliness and need, she had married Carlos. He had been the opposite of Donny, focused on his business, but he had given her Carla, whom she couldn't imagine life without. After Carlos' early death, she had married Billy Rhodes, and had enjoyed a wonderful love affair that had produced her younger daughter, Julie. Billy had not only been a good husband, but a great father to all three of her children, showing no preference toward the only one he actually fathered. They all loved him and they had been a happy family.

Billy's unexpected death from a heart attack had led Sandy to the beach and ultimately to Drake Asher, who was out running errands and she assumed buying her another piece of jewelry. He loved celebrating benchmarks in their life. Dasher, as everyone called him, was a good man. They had a mature relationship. It wasn't as passionate as her life with Donny or Billy had been, but it was steady and fun. He loved her and for that Sandy was grateful. She had begun to worried about him, though. His first wife had died a long slow death that still haunted him in a small way which he never wanted to talk about. Sandy now observed signs that Dasher was slipping mentally. She had not mentioned it to anyone. He had been a brilliant surgeon, and now some days had trouble with words. He would also on occasion take twice as long as necessary to run an errand for her. She suspected that he got lost, but after asking the first time, she had kept her suspicions to herself. He would usually come in the back door in a bad mood which she would just ignore and act as if she didn't notice he was late. A hug and a kiss would return his mood back to the easy-going man she married. When Sandy had asked what he wanted to do for this anniversary, he had replied that since they lived in paradise, he'd like to stay home with her and enjoy her famous beef bourguignon, which was a fancy word for the stew that she made by first braising the beef in red wine. In their short four years, they had been to so many faraway places that Sandy was not unhappy with a quiet night at home. She had bought a special outfit she believed Dasher would appreciate. He always recognized and complimented her when she wore something new.

Sandy was upstairs, out of the shower, dressed in only her underwear, and blow drying her hair when Dasher came in. He walked toward the aromas coming from the kitchen and lifted the lid on the heavy red pot simmering on the stove. It lifted his mood. He hated it when he exited Coastal Grand Mall going the wrong direction. He had driven to North Myrtle Beach before he recognized his mistake. Hopefully, Sandy had been busy with her cooking and hadn't noticed. She probably guessed he had been at Kay Jewelers. She was so beautiful and he loved buying her beautiful things. His first wife had been too practical to appreciate anything she didn't deem necessary. Sandy was so different, so positive and expressive about everything they did together. He was so grateful to have her in his life, buying her gems just added to both of their pleasure. Dasher heard the hair dryer stop   upstairs. He decided to get himself a soda and sit on the porch. He patted the pocket where the gift-wrapped earrings waited for later. He knew Sandy would act surprised, but he also knew she suspected where he had gone.

Dasher was walking toward the door to the porch when it opened. The man who walked through the door was intimidating. His muscles were apparent through his tight, black tee shirt, but his nearly black eyes were more those of a dangerous jungle predator.

Sandy didn't realize Dasher was home until she heard his voice asking someone what they wanted. She threw on a short light-weight robe and started toward the stairs. When she heard the other man's voice she stopped in her tracks. Quietly creeping toward the bedroom door, she peaked through the crack between the door and the frame. The man who jabbed at Dasher's chest was angry and formidable. Sandy picked up her cell phone, put it on mute and looked around the bedroom. Not knowing where to hide, she dropped to the floor and slid under their bed. As the dust ruffle fell back into place, she dialed 911. Told them an intruder was threatening her husband and gave them the address. She then dialed her son-in-law Mike's number, but got voicemail. She gave him the same information and hung up.

"What do you want?" Dasher asked the man walking toward him.

"Where's the guy next door?"

"What?" Dasher asked.

"The guy next door; where is he?"

"No one lives next door," Dasher said.

Sandy covered her mouth to muffle her gasp as she heard the man slap Dasher. She prayed help would come quickly. Where was her dog Hero?

"The guy next door killed my brother and I'm going to make him pay," the intruder snarled.

"There are a couple guys who stay there at times, but mostly it sits empty," Dasher said. "I'm sorry about your brother."

"Shut up and tell me where he is!"

"I told you I don't know," Dasher said. "Please, just leave. I won't even tell anyone you were here."

"Is your wife home?" the man suddenly asked. "She knows him better than you from what I'm told. If you won't tell me, I'll enjoy questioning her, if you know what I mean."

"She's not here," Dasher said. "I just got home and don't know where she is."

Sandy heard another slap that must have knocked Dasher off balance, because she heard the table scratch against the wood floor and a chair fall.

"You lie," the man said, "and I hate liars. Are you going to tell me what I want to know or not?"

"I don't know who you are looking for or where any of those men are. They just come and go. My wife wouldn't know either."

The man pulled a gun from the back of his black jeans, and pointed it at Dasher.

"Stay put or I'll use this on you and your wife both," he said, as he wandered to look into the kitchen.

When the kitchen was empty, his eyes roamed toward the stairway. Dasher had slowly backed up to a small entry table with a drawer which held a handgun. He quietly opened the drawer and withdrew the weapon.

"I told you she isn't home, but you need to leave," Dasher said with authority.

The man snickered and turned to see a gun pointed at him. His bushy eyebrows raised in surprise.

"You've got balls, old man," he said. "Are you going to shoot me?"

"I don't want to, but I will if you don't leave," Dasher said.

Sandy squeezed her eyes shut and swallowed a scream as she heard a gunshot. Where were the police? Had Dasher actually shot someone?

Then she felt herself turn cold with panic. The footsteps coming up the stairs were not Dasher's. The man in black walked to the doorway of her bedroom when sirens could be heard in the distance. He hesitated and then hurried down the stairs. She heard the porch door slam. The sirens became louder as she slipped from under her bed and carefully left the bedroom to look downstairs. The room was empty except for the body of her husband.

"Dasher," she whispered, as her world became dark and she hit the floor.

Dolley Hamilton MacFallon was laughing at a booth at Taproom with Reba and her new neighbor Bella when her phone rang. She started to ignore the call from her husband but suddenly felt it might be important.

"Hey, Mac," she smiled into the phone. "I'm just having lunch with Reba and … What? Where are you? What do you know?"

Dolley listened for a minute and then said. "I need to get there."

"No," Mac said, "Pray until I call you back. I'm headed there and so are the police. I gave Baker a heads up. He's on his way, too."

"Sandy will need me," Dolley said.

"Probably," Mac replied, "but wait until I know the situation. I promise to let you know. Even if she and Drake are alright, she'll want to see you."

"What's your gut tell you?" she asked.

"I'll call you," was all he said before hanging up.

Dolley looked at Reba with fear as their server, Kat, walked up to the table to see how they were doing.

"Sandy called 911 that there was an intruder in their home," she explained.

"Is she okay?" Both Reba and Kat asked.

"Mac doesn't know. He is on his way there now? I should be there, but he said to wait."

"Of course, you should wait," Kat told her.

Dolley quietly prayed. "God, care of our friend. Give her peace and let them be okay."

"Amen," Bella said, before looking from Dolley to Reba. "Does this kind of thing happen often at the beach?" she asked.

"No," Dolley said, "but there has been a little trouble on occasion. Mac will know what to do. He's on his way and alerted Laurie."

"Who's Laurie?" Bella asked.

"He's a detective, and Mac used to be special forces," Reba told her. "They both know how to take care of themselves and neutralize a dangerous situation."

"But you're worried," Bella said.

"Yes," Reba said, "I'm worried."

"You asked about his gut feelings," Bella said to Dolley.

"Mac has an uncommon instinct about these things," Reba explained. "What did he say, Dolley?"

"He didn't answer," Dolley looked at Reba.

"Is that good or bad?"

"I don't think it's good," Dolley answered.

As Kat walked away from the table, Dolley bowed her head and quietly talked to God. Reba and Bella remained quiet.

The little house on the beach in Garden City was approached by two officers with weapons drawn. Their arrival had not been quiet. A man approached them on foot when they pulled up to say that he had heard a gunshot only several minutes before.

"Just one shot?" Detective Baker asked, as Mac MacFallon's car came to an abrupt halt behind his.

"Just one," the man repeated.

"Go back inside and lock your doors," Officer Laurie Baker ordered.

The man ran across the street to the raised beach rental and did as he had been told. Laurie could see three other young adults looking out the front room windows.

"What do we know?" Mac asked.

"Nothing so far," Laurie said, "One shot reported fired. Two officers ahead of us with weapons drawn."

"All clear," one of the advance officers called. "We need a bus."

Mac called for an ambulance as Laurie called for backup to search the area. They both then walked into Sandy's beach house, dreading what they would find.

The first thing they saw was Hero on the porch floor. Laurie walked to him and saw a dart protruding from his fur. He reached down and found the dog to be breathing.

"Tranquilized," he said, both men knowing that was not a good sign.

Laurie led the way into the house. Dasher was on the floor, blood oozing from his chest. One officer called down from upstairs.

"No sign of a struggle upstairs," he said. "The woman appears to have fainted and hit her head. She is not conscious."

Mac ran up to Sandy, passing the officer on the stairs.

"I'm going to check outside," the officer said. "Joe went to check the beach. The guy can't be far."

"I called for backup," Laurie said, "Order a second bus."

"Yes, sir," the officer called as he left the house with his cell phone to his ear.

Laurie could tell Dash was gone, but he still reached down and felt for a pulse in his neck. This job was always hard, but when it was someone you knew … well, it didn't get harder than that. He looked up as Mac talked to Sandy.

"Is she responding?" he asked.

"Not yet, but I believe the officer's assessment was correct," Mac said. "Should I call Dolley to accompany her to the hospital? She'll need someone."

"I'll request a female officer meet them at the hospital," Laurie said. "I'd like the officer to hear Sandy's first recollection of what happened. Dolley can be at the hospital for comfort afterwards."

"Do you think she saw who did this?" Mac asked.

"I both hope she did and pray she didn't," Laurie said.

"I was thinking the same thing," Mac told him.

Chapter 4

Drake Asher's funeral at the beach was solemn. He did not have children, but all of Sandy's were there. The murder had left everyone in shock, and Sandy did not seem to be grieving in the same way she had before. Her children were worried about her. She had always been the emotional and spiritual strength of the family, but it was as if this loss was more than she could handle. They also worried about her safety. The press had not been told that she could identify the shooter, but somehow it had leaked. Mitch wanted her to come home with his family. Sandy refused. If she was in danger, she would not let it spread to his family.

Dolley's heart broke for her friend as she watched her unemotionally receive condolences.

"She'll be okay," Mac said, putting his arm around his wife and kissing her temple. "She'll need time and she'll need you when this is over."

"She should leave the beach until this is over," Dolley said. "Margo offered her a place to stay in Atlanta where no one would be looking for her."

"Margo is probably right that no one would look for her there," Mac said, "but Sandy refuses to put anyone in harm's way. Your friend Margo has a good heart, but she also has a public presence that could put them both in danger."

"I suppose," Dolley said, still watching Sandy across the room. "I find two things interesting. Have you noticed that Longstreet has barely left her side since he got in town?"

"I think he's sleeping on her sofa," Mac said.

Dolley turned surprised eyes to her husband. "He only lives next door," she said.

"Evidently, that's not close enough for him," Mac said. "He has Ike keeping guard with Hero. He said Ike was mentoring Hero for future trouble."

"Hero couldn't help being shot with a tranquilizer," Dolley said.

Mac smiled. "According to Longstreet, the guy wouldn't have had time to shoot a dart before Ike would have reacted to his presence. I think he's probably right. What's the other thing you noticed?"

"Julie's husband, Chris is spending a lot of time talking to Olivia's husband, DJ."

"It seems Chris just finished training under DJ at Quantico," Mac said.

"Did you know that before?" Dolley asked.

"No," Mac said, "But it doesn't surprise me. As a direct-action intelligence trainer, DJ works with a lot of young guys."

"So, Julie's husband wants to be a badass, too?" she ventured.

"From what I hear," Mac said, "He already is."

The family had chosen not to have a big meal for everyone after the funeral. However, around thirty people were invited back to Dolley and Macs for a simple luncheon. The atmosphere relaxed a little due to the presence of children. Olivia had changed into a bathing suit in order to take Sarah into the pool. DJ handed her a floating chair with one-year-old AJ, named after

Allen Longstreet and David's birth father Jacob. DJ smiled at his wife and walked to where Mac sat talking to Sandy's daughter Carla and her husband Mike—the person Sandy had called from under the bed. DJ got himself a beer before sitting down with them.

"How's she doing?" DJ asked Carla.

"I'm worried about her," Carla said. "It's different this time. How much loss can one person take?"

"She's tough," Mac said. "She'll pull through. Death is different when it's violent."

"Longstreet is taking it personally," DJ said. "Who do you think was looking for him?"

"The list would be hard to compile with his background," Mac said.

"Who would be your most logical suspects?" Carla asked.

"I guess since coming to the beach, the main conflicts have been with the Fuentes brothers and then that Myrtle Beach guy who was shot at the airport over trafficking last year," Mike said.

"He had nothing to do with Longstreet," Carla said.

"But he did have something to do with DJ and Rambo who was living next door to Sandy last year," Mike said.

"According to Laurie Baker," Mac added, "They are checking out family of anyone with connection to Sandy, Longstreet, and Rob. Anyone who might have an issue with any of them is being investigated. Laurie said they even went back to the case involving Sandy's friend Patsy, the Realtor who was shot the year she moved here."

"That had nothing to do with Longstreet either," Mike said.

"That's what I told him," DJ said. "It seems the owner of that coffee shop on Atlantic Ave mentioned it to one of the officers."

"Aaron?" Mike responded.

"Yeah, that was his name," DJ said. "Do you know him?"

"He used to go to church and out to lunch with us on occasion. He's pretty low key," Mike said.

"Sometimes people just like to give information to show how important they are," Mac said.

"So, what's the protection detail on Sandy?" DJ asked.

"Longstreet is planning on staying at the beach until the threat has been dealt with," Mac said. "I'm sure she and Dolley will spend a lot of time together, so between the two of us, she won't be alone. Sandy is strong, but it just may take her a while to come back from what she experienced."

"I'm glad Longstreet is staying," DJ said.

"I won't be far from my mother, either," Carla said. "It's good we're working from the beach now instead of being in Asheville."

Above them, Dolley watched the group she loved from her balcony. She loved each of them as though they were blood-related. She didn't know Sandy's son Mitch or her daughter Julie as well as they others, but they were good people, confident and strong. Dolley looked to where Chris and Julie were talking quietly near the gate to the beach.

"Your mother is well protected," Chris said.

"What if she isn't?" Julie asked.

"DJ assured me that the guys around her are the kind that would take a bullet for her, but they don't expect that to happen. They are the kind of men you want protecting her," he smiled.

"Like you," she said.

"Like me," he smiled, and gave her shoulders a squeeze.

"I'm so proud of you and yet I'm afraid," she said.

With his finger, Chris tilted her head up to look him in the eye. He hated to see her fear.

"Why?"

"Why? Because someone is after her, and I know what those men would do to protect her. It's the same thing you do, but this situation with my mother makes me more aware and I hate it."

"What are you saying?" he asked.

She hesitated and shrugged. "I wish you were a barista like that Aaron guy we met at the coffee shop," she smiled.

"Do you really?" he asked skeptically.

"No," she sighed, "I love tough guys. I love a guy who fights for the truth, who stands up for what's right, and who never backs down from doing what's right."

Chris shrugged and smiled with his palms up, as though to say 'that's what you've got'.

"But there's a downside," she said, "I have never been as strong as my mother, and I look at her now and it scares me. I couldn't live if I lost you. Your dad died in combat. Mike was shot, almost died, and had a long rehab. Longstreet and DJ have both had to do long rehab too."

"Tough guys," he smiled, "Mike, DJ, and Longstreet are still the same tough guys they always were. It's an internal thing, Julie. I'm going to do everything in my power to protect you, to have your back, to be there for you—till death do us part. Remember?"

"That's what I'm afraid of," she said as tears threatened.

"Don't be," he said.

Julie buried her face in his chest as her arms tightened around him.

"I don't take unnecessary chances," he quietly said. "None of us do, but if you must know, I've also had a standard, which is why I set my sights on you."

Julie raised her face to look at him.

"I didn't marry a weak insecure girl," he told her. "I married you; a strong woman who loves me, someone that I could count on to be by my side no matter what life brings our way. No one knows the future, Honey. We can't live in fear. God's way is not to live in fear."

"I know that," she said. "I just don't want to ever lose you. I love you, Chris."

"I love you, too," he wrapped both arms around her and held her close. "I am who I am, Julie, the tough guy you married, but I'm not careless. I'll always come home to you. You will be the shining light that brings me home. Most agents never get shot, but if I ever do, you'll be that beaming lighthouse drawing me back to your arms. We'll take care of each other. That's what lovers do. You'll always be that for me, and I'll always be that for you."

As she hugged him, she sighed. She knew he was right and she knew she loved him beyond measure. He would be there for her, and she would be there for him, no matter what the future held. Her mind went back to the pain her mother was again going through. Julie wondered if Sandy had ever loved anyone as much as Julie loved Chris. She believed if she had it was her own father, Billy. Like she and Chris, they had been lovers. That reality gave her a renewed respect for her mother, who she now recognized had gone through that grief alone.   Julie vowed to be more supportive of Sandy this time. After all, Julie wasn't a kid this time. She was a woman who understood love.

Chapter 5

Longstreet sat in the dark holding a cup that had contained black coffee, listening to Sandy moan through another nightmare upstairs. He hated not going to her, but wasn't sure it was appropriate or would even be appreciated. Sandy was determined to show the world that she was handling grief as she always had, with strength and dignity. She would see his concern as overreaching chauvinism. He didn't want to embarrass or insult her, but he hated knowing what she was going through. When he had tried once to tell her that, she had cut off his words by leaving the room.

Suddenly she let out a scream that had his cup hitting the floor as he raced up the stairs. She sat up straight in bed, alone in a semi dark room. Her eyes were not focused on what was real, but on some replay of what might have happened that night. Longstreet rushed to her side and pulled her into his arms. She clung to him, gasping for breath, one hand fisted in his hair. As he rubbed her back and softly reassured her that she was safe, she began to relax. He started to relax his hold on her when the floodgates opened and Sandy began to sob, heart-wrenching, all-consuming sobs that tore at his own heart. Eventually she stilled. Without a word, she moved away from him, and with her back to him, she sighed deeply. He assumed she was embarrassed and she was willing a peaceful sleep to come. He pulled the blanket over her shoulder, and quietly left the room.

Back downstairs, he picked up his cup and walked to the kitchen to fill it. He knew he wouldn't sleep again tonight. Longstreet understood flashbacks and night terrors. He knew how real they were and how they could exhaust a body that had barely moved. Sometimes they were nearly forgotten the next day and other times they enveloped the next day in discouragement or shame. Along with reliving the trauma came the endless questions of responsibility or neglect. Was I responsible in some way? Could I have done something to change the outcome? The doubts seemed hopeless and never-ending. He was sure Sandy had not talked to anyone in detail about that night. It was still bottled up inside of her. Maybe after tonight, he thought as he settled back down on her sofa with the glow of the nearly muted TV casting a blue tint to the room, maybe she'd talk to him. He would let her know he had been there, that he really did understand.

The next morning, a woman that looked much like the Sandy from before the shooting came down the stairs with a bit of a bounce in her step. Her hair was clean and styled and she was wearing makeup, snug jeans, and a fitted tee shirt; not her normal style, but it might be a step in the right direction. He wasn't sure.

"Want me to make fresh coffee?" she asked cheerfully.

"I just did," he said, holding up his mug.

"Then want me to make some breakfast?" she said, stopping before him. "I don't know about you, but I'm starving. Nothing like a good cry to clear the cobwebs and make for a new day!"

"Feeling better, are you?" he asked, still seeing some effects of last night in her eyes. Her lids had soft color and her lashes were curled and mascaraed, but shadows of last night were still evident.

Suddenly serious, she said, "Thank you for last night. I guess I'm not as strong as I thought. I just needed a good cry." When he didn't reply, she added, "I'm glad it was you."

"Me, too," he said. "If you want to make omelets, I'm good at chopping or grating."

Sandy smiled. "You're hired, at double your salary for babysitting me."

"I'm not your babysitter," he said as he stood. "I don't babysit."

As the two dogs looked in from the porch, Longstreet stood, walked to open the door, and added, "Ike and I have been training Hero how to not fall asleep on the job."

Sandy's expression melted as her dog walked to her. She went down to his level and hugged his neck. "I never blamed you," she said. "I know you are brave. I'm sorry you didn't get to show it."

The two adults, followed by the two dogs wandered into the kitchen to fix breakfast. For a while they worked without words. When Sandy finally spoke, it was not what Longstreet expected.

"What kind of person casually kills a man, but goes out of his way not to harm a dog?"

"A sick man," Longstreet said. "When did you know he was in the house?"

"We were supposed to celebrate our anniversary. Dash was gone all afternoon as I prepared one of his favorite dinners. I didn't know he had returned until I turned off my hairdryer and heard his voice as he answered the door. I was about to step out of the bedroom when I realized the man downstairs was angry. I peeked through the crack between the door and the doorframe and saw him."

She stopped talking and began beating the eggs with a fervor.

"Then what?" he quietly asked.

"I don't remember," she said, her zeal for egg beating accelerated.

Longstreet stood and put his hand over hers to stop her effort to kill the eggs. "It's okay," he said.

"No!" she exclaimed, "It's not okay. I was there for his last few minutes of life and I can't even remember them!" Turning sad eyes to him, she asked, "Did he suffer? Was he trying to protect me? Was that what got him killed?"

"I don't think the man was in the house but for a few minutes," Longstreet said. "It appeared he may have hit Drake once. Drake must have somehow retrieved a gun from the open drawer on the hall table."

"Yes," she said, "He kept a gun there."

"The theory is he aimed it at the intruder, but the intruder shot first. There was only one shot that hit his heart. He would not have felt any pain, Sandy. He died instantly from the bullet."

"Thank you," she said, turning the fire on under the burner. "That helps a little. Should we fry some bacon with our eggs?"

There was no more talk about the shooting or the nightmare. She currently didn't remember anymore, but with time he would help her work through the details. She had seen the shooters face, but the shooter didn't know she couldn't remember him yet. Sandy felt better at the moment and wanted normal back in her life. He would help her with that, but talking was the only way it would happen—and Longstreet would see to it that she was never alone until this was over.

Later than afternoon, Carla and Mike sat with Dolley and Mac at Taproom.

"My mom still won't talk to me about what happened," Carla said.

"She will with time," Mac told her.

"But why won't she talk? She was upstairs. It didn't appear that the intruder even knew she was there. She's faced death before."

"Did she talk to you then?" Dolley asked.

"Well, no," Carla admitted, "but we weren't exactly getting along in those days. Now I'm here for her and she won't talk."

"Your mom never experienced what she did this time. Death by sickness or an accident is more explainable. Our minds can make some sense of it. Trauma is different. She has to sort it out before she can put it in words," Mac said.

"But wouldn't talking help her to sort it out?" Carla asked.

"Do you think she knows or remembers what happened?" Mike asked.

"What do you mean? She was there. She must have heard the shot. She told the female officer at the hospital that she saw the shooter's face. Could she forget something like that?"

"Our minds can play tricks on us," Dolley added.

"But you would think she would want to identify the man who murdered her husband so the police could find him," Carla said, pushing her food away and taking a sip from her glass of wine.

"Is it survivor's guilt?" Dolley asked Mac.

"It could be; irrational guilt that she didn't stop it. Maybe she believes she brought this trouble upon Drake and if it weren't for her, he would still be alive," Mac told her.

"That's ridiculous," Carla said.

"I'm just saying it could be a lot of things. She just may have blacked out the entire episode because it is too hard to think about. If you can't remember it, you don't have to process it," Mac concluded.

"Give her time," Mike said, putting his hand on Carla's arm.

"I just want to help her," Carla sighed. "I feel so helpless. I could maybe aid in finding this guy if she would give us something to go on. If nothing else, she would have heard what he said to Dasher. Anything she could remember would move us forward. We have almost nothing."

"We do know he claimed to be looking for the man who killed his brother," Mike said.

"And I've exhausted every relative I can find for anyone the police think could be connected to mom or Longstreet in any way. If she told the officer at the hospital the shooter was looking for a man, why would Mom feel responsible?" Carla asked.

"Be patient, Carla," Dolley said, sympathetically. "She's got to be struggling with all of this. I'm sure if she tells Longstreet anything, he'll let you know. He's sticking to her like glue. No one's going to hurt her. You'll find the guy, or the police will. I'm praying for that end as I pray my friend finds peace in all of this.

It can't be easy for her. I'm going over there tomorrow to see if she'll come to my house for a swim. Longstreet said she hasn't left the house since the day after the funeral, but this morning she came downstairs with makeup and her hair fixed and wanted to cook breakfast. She'll heal in her own time. We can pray for her as she does."

Chapter 6

The next morning, Carla walked into the office of Longstreet Campbell Investigations and Forensic Lab. She juggled three coffees and a box of banana walnut scones.

"These are amazing," Will stated as he bit into one before taking his coffee out of her hands.

"I could use a little help before the box and coffees end up on the floor," Carla said.

"Oh, sure. Sorry," he smiled, taking two of the coffee cups with the second half of his scone hanging out of his mouth.

"Your mother was not good at teaching manners," Carla scoffed. "Is Mike in yet?"

"Don't you two live together?" Will asked, grabbing a second scone and heading toward his office.

"We even sleep in the same bed," she stated, "but he left early this morning and said he'd see me at the office."

"Haven't seen or heard from him," Will called.

Carla rolled her eyes. Having an attorney working from their office had brought a fair deal of business to their young company, but it still surprised her that his business kept growing. She accepted the fact that he was very smart and knew the law, but sometimes he reminded her of a teenage boy. She put her coffee on her desk and walked to the lab.

"What time did you get here?" she asked the only other person in the building, handing him his large, double caf/extra sugar latte, with no whip/extra foam.

"I came in around 3am," Andrew Carney, the forensic analysis said without looking up. "Thanks for my first of the day." He toasted her in the air with the coffee she handed him.

"Couldn't sleep?"

"Nope," he said, finally leaning back and taking a sip of his drink. "How's your mom doing?"

"Slow process," she said. "Is that the Kauffman case that won't let you sleep?"

"Yep," he said, standing to stretch and walk around the room several times before sitting back down. "Come look at this."

Carla walked over and looked over his shoulder at his computer screen. "What am I looking for?"

"A routine payment that seems a little high for a monthly contribution."

"Are you referring to line 27?"

"Yep."

"So, he makes a lot of money and donates a lot to the Red Cross. Maybe he likes the deduction, or he's a crook with a soft heart for disasters."

"Look at it more closely," he said.

"$2700 a month. Like I said he believes in the Red Cross. That's from his personal account, isn't it?"

"Yes, it is and he never takes the donations on his taxes, even though every one of his locations gives the same $2700 monthly."

"That's over $32,000 a year per location!" Carla exclaimed. "What's the deal?"

"Read the name of the organization one more time, slowly," Andrew smiled.

"Red Cruss," she read. "Is it a typo on the bank leger?"

"In ten different locations? That's $340,000 a year—to a typo? I looked up "Red Cruss. It's an LLC registered in the name of Theodore Kauffman." Andrew explained.

"A brother? Cousin?" Carla asked.

"The only Theodore Kauffman I could locate is his seven-year-old son. He opened the account the year he was born. $2700 a month from each location has given our accountant friend a whopping total of $2,268,000 before interest in tax free money!"

"How is it tax free?" she asked.

"Because no one, including the government, knows who or where Red Cruss is. He has been flying under the radar all these years. I'm actually kind of impressed."

"Don't go getting any ideas," she said as she flicked his shoulder with her thumb and middle finger.

"I work for pastries, remember?" he smiled, leaning back and looking very proud of himself. "What kind did you bring me today?"

"Scones," she said, as she left the lab. "My coffee's getting cold."

As Carla got back to the front of the offices, a delivery came packed in dry ice just as their lab tech who she affectionately called Ben came through the front door. As Carla signed for the box of specimens, Ben picked up the box, and with his backpack strapped to his athletic body, he said, "Morning Boss. How's your mom doing?"

"Still struggling, Ben."

"Give her time," he said.

"I don't seem to have a choice," she answered.

At 11:00 am, Mike came in and went straight to his office. At 11:25, she poked her head in his door and said she was going to lunch. He nodded and kept listening to whoever was on the phone. Since all her workers were in separate offices absorbed in their own work, Carla locked the front door as she left. There was a bell and a note to ring it if the door was locked during working hours. Carla walked to her car and drove to Taproom.

When Carla walked through the door, Tap walked over and gave her a hug.

"How are things going?" he asked.

"As well as can be expected," she smiled. Looking around she spotted her friends. "I see I'm the last one here."

"What are you drinking?" he asked. "I'll send it over."

"An Arnold Palmer," she said, "Thanks, Tap."

Carla walked to the table where Marti, Rose, Elsa, and Reba awaited her. Marti stood and also gave her a hug. The others looked either sympathetic or concerned.

"How are you?" Rose asked.

"I'm doing okay," she responded.

"How's Sandy?" Elsa said once Carla was seated.

"Struggling," Carla said.

"How many times must she go through loss?" Reba stated.

"This time is different, isn't it?" Elsa said. "I could tell at the funeral."

"It is different this time," Carla said. "I'm a little worried about her."

"It's Sandy," Marti said. "She has a strong faith that will carry her through. It must have been horrible to see your husband shot."

"That's just it," Carla said, "She didn't see it happen, or if she did, she doesn't remember."

"I read that she saw the killer," Reba added. "That has to be terrifying."

"She doesn't remember any of it," Carla said.

"But if the killer thinks she does, she could be in danger," Reba responded.

Carla nodded. "Longstreet is at her side. He won't let anything happen to her."

Barb appeared with Carla's drink and one of her own. She took the last seat at the table.

"Longstreet stayed in town?" she asked, as she sat across from Carla.

"Yes. He'll keep her safe." She took a sip of her drink and smiled. "In fact, he's been trying to teach Hero to be a guard dog. He keeps telling him he has to live up to such a big name."

"How's that going?" Marti smiled, "Hero would rather be a cuddler than a fighter."

"I think that's what Longstreet is finding out, but he's determined to advance Hero's protective skills," Carla said. "I have to admit that it's pretty impressive. He's using Ike, and Hero tries to be like Ike, at least for a while. I was watching them one morning. Hero responds well to commands until he tires of the game and wants to become a spectator."

The girls chuckled.

"Does Longstreet think he can teach him to attack?"

"I think Longstreet would settle with him becoming a better watchdog and sounding more ferocious. Hero will never be Ike. Ike was trained by the Army as a pup."

"Ike actually scares me," Marti said.

"He's supposed to," Carla said. "Fluffy, happy Hero will never look scary, but Longstreet is determined to make a protector out of him. He really does keep challenging him to live up to his name. It's kind of funny to watch."

"So, who do you think is more determined?" Elsa asked, "the trainer or the dog?"

"I'm not sure," Carla responded.

"Can we do anything to help Sandy?" Rose asked.

"I think for now, she's mostly open to time alone and time with Dolley. You can continue to pray for her."

"Knowing someone might want you dead cannot be easy," Elsa said. "I know she's not afraid to die."

"Some days it almost seems like she longs for it," Carla said, "but I'm trusting it is just part of the process."

"We'll keep praying for her and reaching out in texts," Barb said.

"I believe that's all you can do for now," Carla agreed. "I appreciate all of you, more than you know."

Kat came over to take their orders. When she left the table conversation resumed.

"How's our famous mystery writer doing?" Carla asked Reba. "Is the book still selling off the shelves?"

Reba smiled. "Sales have slowed down, which is expected, but they haven't stopped. The fact that it was a true story makes people want to read it."

"The fact that you're a great writer doesn't hurt," Marti smiled, as heads around the table nodded in agreement.

"It's nice having such supportive friends," she said. "I was approached this week about allowing a scriptwriter to turn the book into a movie script."

Exclamations rang out around the table.

"Wow!"

"That is amazing!"

"I talked to Will about it and he has asked me not to take that path."

"Why not?"

"I can understand that," Barb said. "It's a little like Sandy's situation. I wouldn't want any more publicity if I were Will, either."

"But the book is already out," Rose said.

"Yes, but with time the story will fade. It will always be a good book," Barb qualified, "but not always newsworthy. I'd hate to have my story as a lifetime movie for everyone to watch and think they know all about me. A movie is just that—a movie."

"I've gotten to know Will now that he works for us," Carla said, "and I'm not surprised. He's pretty low-key. I went to court one day and sat at the back to watch him in action. He's good at what he does, but he's modest for an attorney, even though he appears strong in the courtroom."

"I like him," Marti said.

"Of course, you do," her cousin Barb replied.

"What's that supposed to mean?" Marti asked.

"You like men," Barb stated simply.

"And you don't?" Marti challenged.

"At this stage of my life, they're not high on my priority list."

"You should start dating," her cousin told her.

"That's the last thing I should do," Barb said.

"I have to agree with Barb on this," Elsa said. "Being a single mom with an ex can't be easy. We're all here to keep her from getting lonely."

"You're not all there in the night-time hours," Marti said.

"I sleep in the night-time hours," Barb told her. "It's my only time that's just for me. I need that to recharge for another day."

"So, how's the business coming?" Rose asked Carla to change the subject.

"Better than we even expected," she replied. "I think we can thank Detective Baker for giving us such high praise that we are used regularly by the local police forces. Then we were able to hire this quirky lab technician who works miracles with each new machine we are able to obtain. He's fun to watch and he sees things other people don't."

"I heard that Taylor wants to join forces with you guys," Elsa said. "She and Olivia keep in touch."

"Yes. Taylor finished her nursing degree, but went right back to school to acquire a master's degree in forensic science. It seems it piggybacks onto the science she learned for nursing," Carla said.

"Well, she is one of the most curious people I've come across," Rose said. "Sometimes her questions bordered on intrusive."

"Probably what will make her good at forensics," Carla said. "It will be interesting to see how she and Ben fit into the same lab, but he will need help as business grows."

The balance of lunch was easy conversation between friends. At one point, they were telling Reba, the newest member of the group, old stories that had everyone laughing. As Carla drove back to work, she realized that had been exactly what she needed—a break from the sadness of loss and danger.

When Carla got back to the office, she was greeted by an excited Ben who had new information. He had gone by the police station to look over the almost zero amount of evidence they had from Drake Asher's murder.

"Carla," he said, "You owe some expensive tickets to an officer named Larry Graham. He happened to notice with all the footprints in the sand that one pair indicated that someone had jumped over the railing from your mom's porch and run toward the ocean. He took pictures and even made a mold of one right and one left print that were clear enough."

"How do you make a print in sand? It shifts if you just blow on it," she asked.

"I'm not sure," Ben said, "He claims his secrets gives him employment security."

"Okaaayy," she replied. "So, this print shows a shoe that is special in some way?"

"Not the shoe exactly, the gait," Ben said. "See how the foot doesn't step evenly in the sand. It seems like the guy walks on the side of his foot?"

"Are you sure that's not just because he's walking in sand? I walk differently in sand than on a hard surface," she said.

"Look how it not only is heavier on one side of his foot than the other, but the heal part of the print is light and the toe part is deeper."

"I'm not seeing what you're seeing," she said.

"A limp," he said, and stood up to demonstrate.

Ben walked around the room with a specific gait that was leaning on the outside of his left foot with an emphasis of putting his weight more on his toes than his heel.

When he walked back to her, he said, "See. Your suspect is able to jump over a railing and probably run down the beach, but he has a bit of a limp when he walks. Was your stepdad missing a jacket and hat after the attack? I'll bet he covered his black shirt your mother said he was wearing and looked like any jogger running on the beach. I'll bet he's on the younger side, too."

"Why?"

"Because a limp like this is not from an injury or old age. It's something someone has compensated for his whole life. My guess is it is more exaggerated when he is tired and/or not consciously trying to control it. People who only know him casually may never even notice it, but it's there"

"It's not much, but it's something," Carla said. "Thanks, Ben. I'm not sure anyone but you and Officer Graham would have ever seen it. I'll owe you both a bonus when we catch this guy."

"A bonus?" he grinned.

"Well, at least a gold star," she smiled, and walked back to her desk.

Chapter 7

Two weeks later, Carla got a call from Dolley.

"Next Tuesday is Elsa's birthday," she stated. "I'm planning a birthday luncheon for her. Your mom said she would come."

"Good," Carla said, looking at her schedule. "I'm free. Where are we meeting?"

"I'm thinking of just having everyone at my house. I'll see if Rose and Elsa can get sitters and Barb can schedule time off. I'd like it to be a nice girls' day out."

"That will be fun," Carla said. "How can I help?"

"I've got everything covered. I'll make lunch, order a cake, and pick up balloons."

Carla laughed. "You and your balloons! You even had balloons at Olivia's wedding."

"I like balloons. They make people smile. They make an event more festive," Dolley argued.

"I guess they do," Carla said. "I heard DJ and Olivia may come in this weekend for Elsa's birthday. You might check with them about Tuesday. See if they can stay long enough for Olivia to join us."

"Does Elsa know they are coming in or is it a surprise?" Dolley asked.

"I'm not sure," Carla responded. "Mike told me. Do you have Olivia's new number?"

"No."

"I'll text it to you," Carla said. "Thanks for planning this. Let me know if I can do anything."

"I will," Dolley said.

The following Tuesday was beautiful. The temperature was in the high 80's and the blue skies over the ocean behind Dolley's house had scattered white clouds; just enough to make the sky picture-perfect.

Elsa and Olivia walked in a little late, and were greeted by all of their friends along with Bella. Reba had asked if she could bring Bella to meet the group. Bella was easy to talk to and fit in immediately. Everyone had made arrangements to be able to come, so, besides Dolley, Sandy, Carla, Reba and Bella, there was Rose, Barb, and Marti to greet the birthday girl and her daughter. The ten women of various ages and walks of life were happy to be together, and especially happy to have Sandy with them. They each had given her an extra-long hug, but otherwise made the day about anything other than her loss and current situation.

Dolley's great room was big enough to easily accommodate the group. After lunch, they lounged comfortably, sharing life stories of the past and their current situations. Carla had been asked about her business. Reba, her book sales. Olivia, her new life at Quantico. They purposefully avoided Sandy's danger and Barb's divorce. Marti was able to entertain them concerning the latest event she planned back in Texas at the ranch of an oil tycoon.

"You live a charmed life," Rose said. "I've never been to Texas, but Tap likes to watch westerns, so I think I know what it looks like."

"Mac watches those, too," Dolley said, "but Texas has big cities, and I've heard that the Austin area is actually green hills with trees."

"I spent a little time in Texas," Carla said. "It's where Mike and I met."

"That's right," Marti said, "You were a runaway."

"I was not a runaway," Carla informed her. "I was on a mission."

"A mission that almost got me killed," Dolley reminded her with a smile.

"Okay," she conceded, "not one of my finest hours, but it did lead to my finest decision." She put her hand in the air wiggling the finger that supported her wedding rings."

"That sounds like a fascinating story," Bella said. "You'll have to fill me in sometime."

"Tell us your story," Carla said. "We all know each other's; we've lived through much of them."

Bella looked around the room. "Are you sure you want to hear it?" she asked.

"Of course," Dolley encouraged.

"Well," she smiled. "Here goes. I spent the first ten years of my life as Isabella Briggs, the happy only child of Jameson Briggs, a missionary from Colorado who fell in love with and married Mariana Torres. I was born the next year, and we lived in the town of Alamos in Sorona, Mexico; a small town dating back to the 1600's when silver mines were discovered there."

"That's amazing," Marti said. "How did you end up here at the beach."

"Will you let her talk?" Carla said.

"I'm just encouraging her," Marti replied.

"I loved my life in Mexico," Bella continued. "When my Grandma Lettie Briggs, came to visit and said it was time for her granddaughter to come live with her, there was a family feud. My mother did not want to let me go. In the end, Grandma won, as she always does. She said God told her I was to finish school in the United States and learn of my Western American heritage. It was hard to argue with Grandma when she would quietly explain that God had told her. The month after we left Mexico, seven men with masks and weapons knocked down my parent's door, accusing them of stealing drugs from the Cartel. Obviously, they had the wrong house, but by the time they discovered their mistake, they had raped my mother, beaten my father, and killed them both. If Grandma hadn't already taken me to America, I would have suffered the same fate. I'm grateful to God and Grandma for saving me."

"So, you grew up with your grandparents in Colorado?" Marti asked.

"Yes," Bella said, "the next eight years were spent near Pueblo, Colorado on 40 acres owned by my grandparents where I learned to care for horses, plant and harvest a garden, cook and entertain guests. After high school graduation I attended and graduated from John Brown University, in Siloam Springs, Arkansas, before returning to Pueblo to assist Grandma Lettie in caring for my ailing grandfather while taking online courses that earned me a master's degree in literature."

"So, how did you end up here?" Marti probed.

"I loved my life in Colorado. I had recently started dating a professor at Colorado State University when God told Grandma

Lettie that I was supposed to move to the East coast and write novels."

"Are you serious?" Marti asked.

"I told my grandmother that I didn't know if I had enough imagination to write fiction, but she scolded me for not having any faith. I had faith," she continued. "I believed in two things. One, that God was real and had a plan for my life, and two, that when He gave instructions to Grandma Lettie, they were meant to be followed. I was only alive because God had told Grandma Lettie to bring me to the ranch."

"So, she moved next door to me," Reba finished, "and now she has to find that novel in her head that Grandma Lettie told her to write."

"If it were only as easy as Reba makes it sound," Bella laughed.

"Well, you have a good mentor," Rose said. "We all loved Reba's book, and she came here in much the same way."

"That's what she told me," Bella said, "And now I have a new set of friends and a new life to begin." Turning to Carla she said, "I'd like to know more about your lab. Would it be possible to have a tour sometime? It might spark a story in me."

"Sure," Carla agreed. "We'll set up a time. I'll introduce you to my quirky team. I believe setting up our business was a God thing, also. We would have never found the amazing staff we have on our own. God just seemed to bring them to us."

"Tell me about one of your adventures," Bella said.

"Well," Carla looked to the birthday girl, "I think Elsa should tell you how she and Olivia first met the guy who is now

Elsa's husband. We all know her story, but it's fun to hear it again."

As Elsa recounted being homeless and meeting Tap after Olivia passed out from a date-rape drug in Taproom, Carla watched her mother. Sandy seemed more her old self today than she had since Dash's murder. Carla exchanged looks with Dolley who she knew was thinking the same thing. She wished they had more clues to go on to help her mother move forward from her loss—again.

The following morning when Tap entered the Taproom kitchen for his morning coffee, Russ told him that he saw Jake sneaking out of the upstairs apartment.

"Is Barb still there?" Tap asked of the upstairs apartment that was currently not rented to anyone.

"I haven't heard her leave," Russ said, pulling the makings for today's special from the commercial refrigerator.

Tap hesitated, before walking up the back stairs with two coffees, and knocking on the door to the apartment he owned.

"Hey," he said when Barb opened the door.

"Hey Tap," she smiled sheepishly. "I asked Marty to spend the night with the kids. I needed some space. I should have asked permission, but I knew no one was living here now. I put clean sheets on the bed."

"Can we talk?"

"Sure. Is something wrong at the restaurant?" she asked.

"No. Everything is fine. I brought you a coffee," he said, holding up the cup he had poured for her.

The two of them entered the tiny kitchen and sat on stools at the counter.

"What's going on?" she asked.

"I was just wondering the same thing," Tap said, quietly. "Russ said it looked like you and Jake both spent the night in the apartment."

"Right to the point, as usual. Yes, he spent the night at the apartment with me, not that it's any of your business," she said.

When he looked mildly surprised, she added, "Did you think I'd lie to you?"

"You never have before," he said. "Are you two getting back together?"

Barb smiled, "I think so, Tap. He's being so sweet and repentant. The kids will be thrilled to see him. He's apologized for everything."

"What happened between he and Claire?" he asked.

"You remembered her name?" Barb asked with surprise.

"Of course, I remember her name," he said, "She's the woman he cheated with and broke your heart."

"And now he's back and I've forgiven him," Barb said. "You should be happy for me, Tap. I want you to be happy for me."

"I want to be, Barb, but I'm worried he's going to break your heart again. How will that effect Josh? What happened with Claire?"

"I didn't ask," she said.

"You didn't ask?"

"Tap. I want my marriage to work. I love Jake. Doesn't the Bible say we are to forgive? Isn't that what grace is all about?"

"Yes," Tap says, "but putting up boundaries to protect your children and your own heart is not a bad thing."

"He said he'd come to church with us," she smiled. "He's different. You used to really like Jake."

"He hurt you, Barb," Tap said. "I can't tell you what to do, but don't make it too easy for him to walk in and out of your life. It's not love if he only wants you when he needs you."

"That's not fair," Barb said.

Tap took a sip of his coffee. "Maybe it's not," he said, "Do you trust me?"

"Of course," she said, "but my life is my life."

"I agree with that, and it's not my place to tell you what to do, but you are not only my business partner, you're the little sister I never had. I feel protective of you, and I would have more respect for Jake if he had asked you to dinner, not crawled back into your bed."

"He's still my husband as far as I'm concerned," she defended.

"Is he still behind on child support?"

"He promised to catch me up on that, Tap," she said. "He was so sweet last night. He wants us to be a family. He's got a new job."

"Does it involve travel?" Tap asked.

"Some," she replied, not understanding the meaning behind his question, "but he promised to be home as much as possible."

"Home?" Tap responded, "So, he's moving back in?"

"He will be," she smiled. "Don't be mad at me, Tap." She put her hand over his. "I love him and I want our family back together. I want to trust him, so don't make it hard for me."

"Make him talk to you, Barb," he said.

"What?"

"Make him tell you why he left you and then why he left Claire. Ask him where he would be living if you asked him to take this reconciliation slowly. Maybe you should start with dating and building trust, without just jumping in with both feet."

"Jake's not like you," she said, "It's hard for him to talk about things like feelings, but I know he loves me. He said he can't wait to see the kids. He's missed them as much as they've missed him."

"He just has to call and you not only forgive him, but you make it easy for him to take you to bed," he said, not hiding his distrust and irritation.

"We went to bed *together*! It was a mutual decision. God, Tap! You have no idea what it's like to love someone and not be able to be with them. I needed him as much as he needed me."

Tap didn't respond for a minute. Then he gave Barb a small smile and said, "I want what is best for you and the kids. You know I love all of you. I just don't want to see you hurt again. Be careful, Barb. Think about the kids. Guard your heart."

"Tap," she smiled, "Love is about giving your heart, not guarding it."

"It's about both," he said.

She finished her coffee and stood. "I have an hour before we open. I'll see you later."

Barb picked up the sheets that she was taking home to wash, and looked at her boss and friend. "I know you think you're looking out for me, but I'm a big girl. I know what I'm doing."

Tap smiled and watched her leave the room. The last part of her statement sounded more hopeful than confident. He had hired Jake off the streets years ago. He had watched him grow up into what he had thought was a responsible man, but he was wary of the person he had become. Sometimes it was too easy to fall back into old habits. Tap didn't trust him at this point, but he realized, like Barb, he wanted to. Everyone deserved a second chance. He would have been more optimistic, however, if their first reunion had been out in the open instead of sneaking behind closed doors.

Chapter 8

"Hey," Carla greeted Longstreet as he entered the office doors Friday morning. "Where's Mom?"

"Mac just took her and Dolley to the Carolina Wellness Spa for the day," he replied.

"The Massage and Cryo place?" she asked.

"I guess so," he said. "Dolley signed them up for the whole package."

"Wow. I'm surprised. That will be good for her, although I'm shocked," she agreed. "I don't think she's ever had a spa treatment, but then there were years when I was younger that I didn't pay much attention to my mother. I regret that now."

"Water under the bridge," Longstreet said in his matter-of-fact manner. "Does Andrew have anything new?"

"I just got in a bit ago, but he looks like he might have been here all night. The guy never sleeps."

"Military," was all Longstreet said as he headed toward the forensic analyst's office.

"Carney," Longstreet said, as he walked through the inner office door.

"Longstreet," the focused analyst replied.

"Got anything new?" Longstreet asked.

Andrew pulled himself away from his computer screen and smiled. "Have a seat," he said.

Longstreet took that as good news, sat, and waited for Andrew to explain.

After a dramatic pause, Andrew said, "I don't think it was the Fuentes brothers."

"Why not?"

"I can't find anyone directly connected to them with a lingering interest in what happened here. They all seem to have moved on to other ventures, some legal, some questionable, but no connection to this side of the country."

"You used the word directly," Longstreet said.

Andrew's smiled widened. "Yes, I did. Does the name Clark Creek ring any bells?"

"Also known as Clark Vegas," Longstreet said. "Suspected to be in illegal transactions with Marsha Barclay."

"Also known as Marsha Vegas," Andrew said.

"Related?" Longstreet asked.

"Can't find any blood ties. Clark was born a Creek, not a Vegas. Haven't found the reason to align with that family yet. But I do know he was at the beach the week before the murder."

"The week before," Longstreet restated.

"Yes," Andrew said, "He's not your killer, but he could have paid a local and gone back to Colorado to divert any attention to himself."

"Why would he be after me?" Longstreet asked.

"Not sure who he was after … if it was him. Still searching every lead, but when his name popped up, my attention was turned in his direction. Were you part of that art theft that was thwarted?"

"Not really," he said. "That was more Mac's involvement. His now wife, Dolley, was abducted by the Fuentes brothers, one of whom was killed in a motorcycle accident trying to outrun capture."

"And the Fuentes brothers were involved with Fine Jewelry, owned by Marsha Barclay, nee Vegas?" Andrew said.

"Yes, but the stolen art could never be directly connected to her. She's never been linked to corruption, just suspected of it many times," Longstreet said. "She's a smart lady."

"Well, she's on my radar now," Andrew said, "and maybe not that smart if she's after you instead of Mac. Never had any other run-ins with her?"

"Not that I'm aware, but I've been involved in a lot of cases over the years. If she hides that well, maybe I missed something. I'll look back over anything connected to Colorado."

"I'm afraid," Andrew cautioned, "it could be a connection just about anywhere. Her tenacles seem to reach far and wide."

"Tenacles?" Longstreet smiled.

"Like a cephalopod, a cousin to the octopus," Ben said, as he entered the room with his coffee. "They have multiple tenacles that are used to capture prey, but retract back onto their shell, making them look innocuous."

"Okay," Longstreet said. "So where else do Marsha's tenacles reach?"

"A lot of places," Andrew said, "I'll see if I can put together a list, but it won't be as extensive as her reach. The woman flies under the radar, but she's powerful and tenacious. She's not driven by ego. She can walk away from people or profit if she believes her concerns might be compromised. She's too big to care about things like revenge, but everyone makes a mistake. Everyone has an Achilles heel. I'll keep looking for hers."

"But you suspect she's behind Asher's murder?" Longstreet said.

"She's a thread to pull," Andrew said. "Nothing is really solid enough to call a lead yet."

Longstreet left the business that still carried his name feeling a little better. It wasn't anything concrete, but it was an avenue to explore. It was more than he had when he went there. Once in his car, he called DJ at Quantico to see if DJ's new forensic buddy there could do a deep dive into Marsha Barclay.

"Who was that guy?" Bella asked as she was greeted by Carla and Mike in the lobby of their office.

They both smiled, as Carla introduced her husband to Bella Briggs, Reba's new neighbor.

"Nice to meet you," they said in unison as they shook hands.

"That was Allen Longstreet," Carla said, "my mom's neighbor."

"The guy watching over her?" Bella asked. "No wonder she feels secure. He looks intense."

"Let's just say she's safe," Mike said. "You ladies have a nice afternoon."

As Mike left the office, Carla walked Bella back to the conference room. She offered Bella something to drink, and then they both sat at the end of the long table with bottles of water.

"So," Carla began, "Did you really come here for a tour, or is there something else you needed?"

Bella smiled. "I came for the tour," she said. "The idea of a forensic lab sounded like something from a spy movie. I thought it might trigger a story, or maybe you could give me an idea for a story."

"You really plan to write a novel because your grandmother said God told her you should?"

"Crazy, huh?"

"What would you be doing if you weren't following someone else's directions for your life?"

"I don't really know," Bella said.

"Don't be offended, but do you really have a master's degree in literature?"

"I am offended," Bella responded, "Why would you question that?"

"I'm not sure," Carla answered, "I sometimes just feel the need to ask questions."

"Like your friend Marti?" Bella said.

Carla smiled. "Marti's just nosey."

"And what do you call yourself?" Bella asked.

"Curious, probing, a good investigator," Carla said. "I often go down paths even I don't understand."

"So, you thought I was lying about my degree? It was done online and I can produce my credentials if you need them," Bella replied.

"No," Carla said, "I asked you not to be offended. I just felt the need to ask."

"It was offensive," Bella said, "but I'll chalk it up as an unsavory quality of your profession and let it go."

"Fair enough," Carla said. "This is our conference room, the only space where we have room to meet all together or with clients. I have an office and so does Mike. Our forensic analyst has an office filled with computer equipment and our forensic lab is a room filled with scientific equipment that analyzes everything from blood to … well, everything. What questions can I answer for you before I give you the tour?"

"You said you work with local police," Bella commented.

"Yes, they use us because we can get results back to them quickly."

"Are you open to the public?"

"We do mandated drug tests for individuals or companies," Carla said. "We sometimes do blood tests, but those are usually handled by labs connected to medical facilities."

"Longstreet isn't law enforcement, is he?" Bella said.

"No," Carla said, "He's ex-military and a friend. He just stopped by to see Mike."

"Can I see the lab, or is that top-secret stuff?"

"I'll show you the lab and introduce you to Dr. Mark Bennett," Carla said, as she stood.

The two of them walked past the open door to Andrew's office. He didn't look up as they passed. When they got to Ben's closed door, Carla knocked.

"Enter," he called from the other side.

As they did so, he removed a contraption that looked like a gas mask from his face.

"Oh, don't be alarmed," he said, seeing Bella's expression. "I was just being cautious, but this stuff is harmless. I promise."

"Dr. Bennett," Carla said, "This is Bella Briggs. She requested a tour of our offices."

Keeping with Carla's formality, he removed his latex glove and reached out to shake her hand. "How do you do," he replied.

Hesitantly, Bella shook his hand.

"Is your company considering using our services?" he asked as he removed the other glove and tossed both into a nearby open bin.

"Bella is a novelist looking for inspiration," Carla said.

"I thought I might get an idea for a story from seeing this place in person," she smiled.

"I assume you write police thrillers?" Ben said. "I'm working on a case involving a mysterious poison. It was first ruled an accident, but the family pushed for further lab work which discovered a poison called thallium. It is colorless, odorless, and tasteless, making it hard to identify."

"But you identified it?"

"I did," he smiled. "It's what I do. I would think it's a good one to use in a mystery book."

"What are the symptoms?" she asked.

"Gastrointestinal," he said. "Nausea, vomiting, abdominal pain. It is easily diagnosed as a harmless illness like the flu."

"How long does it take to kill someone?" she asked.

"Oh, probably five to seven days on average. It eventually shuts down the respiratory system."

"Thanks," Bella smiled. "That's an idea that I will write down. I'm just beginning the idea of a book, so any new knowledge is helpful. What's that large machine over there?" she asked, pointing across the room.

Ben answered, without walking her to the machine. "That's a mass spectrometer. That's what analyzes anything chemical. I depend on it daily."

"It's all very interesting," Bella said. "Thank you, Dr. Bennett. I'll let you get back to work. You have given me an idea with your poison information."

"You're welcome," Ben said, and turned back to the table he had been working at.

Carla led Bella back to the lobby. Bella thanked her and left. Carla liked Reba, but warming up to Bella was not going to be easy. She wasn't sure why.

As she walked back to her office, Ben met her in the hallway.

"What was that all about?" he asked.

"I met her at a friend's house and she asked for a tour."

"Dr. Bennett?"

"That is your name," she answered.

"But you have never called me that, except the day the police chief stopped by."

"It felt right," Carla shrugged.

"You don't like her or you don't trust her?" Ben asked.

"Maybe neither," she said, "You know me. I just got a gut feeling. It's probably nothing. She seems nice and everyone else at the party warmed up to her. Sometimes it takes me longer than the rest."

"Did you warm up to me right away?" he asked with a smile.

"I'm still deciding about you," she said, returning his smile, "but the odds are in your favor."

"Good to know, Boss," he said, and headed back to his lab.

Carla wondered what it was about Bella. She considered looking into her past, but decided against it. Digging up dirt from people's pasts was not a good pastime when it came to personal relationships. She had the skills, but believed everyone was entitled to past mistakes and second chances. Her life was a testimony to that. She knew no one who didn't have at least some small infraction to hide. She decided she'd bury her suspicions concerning Bella Briggs since she had no idea what had prompted them. She was in all likelihood a lovely woman with a difficult past. That was something Carla usually admired. She would give Reba's friend the benefit of the doubt ... at least for now.

Chapter 9

Sandy sighed as she came downstairs and found her home to herself. She wasn't sure what to call what she was going through, part grief, part fear, part frustration. At the beginning she had been comforted by Longstreet's constant presence, but as she felt better, it had become draining. It surprised her that she felt that way, because in the old days … well, the old days were different. She was sure she had been different then, and she knew Longstreet was. It didn't feel so much like a friendship these past weeks. It felt more like she was a job to him, and she hated that feeling. He showed more affection to Hero than he did to her. He was all business, and she was tired of being someone's project. She couldn't have her life with Dasher back, but she would find a way to get the old Sandy back.

The problem was that the old Sandy had limited memory of the night Dash was killed, and that made her angry. As new memories came to mind, little bits and pieces of that awful evening would pop into focus. She would tell them to Longstreet and he would praise her for remembering but then say little or nothing. There had been a time when they could talk for hours about nothing. It was almost as if they had never had that relationship. She certainly didn't have that closeness now. There had been nights right after the murder when Sandy would have liked a comforting shoulder to cry on, but Longstreet never offered. Except the night when she had the vivid nightmare and she had sobbed in his arms. But that guy didn't show up again. When it came to consoling her, he had been a one-hit-wonder, as the saying goes.

During these weeks of seclusion, Sandy had wrecked her brain for someone that wanted to hurt her or Dasher. Actually, the intruder never threatened Dasher for anything except information. She wondered if Dasher hadn't drawn a gun on him if he'd still be alive. Except, the intruder had been on the stairs when Dash fired, which meant he died protecting her—and for what? She didn't have any enemies. The intruder had wanted information on the man living next door. That had to be Longstreet or Rob, who went by the nickname Rambo. He stayed there sometimes and had probably been the target; someone named Rambo had to collect enemies everywhere he went. Longstreet told her they had ruled out the Fuentes brothers who had caused so much trouble years ago. Who else could possibly still be after her? No one! Longstreet still slept on the sofa at night, but was now going to his house next door during the day, leaving Ike and Hero with her. She would be happy to spend time with the old Longstreet, but this stoic one was more annoying than comforting.

Longstreet heard Sandy's porch door open and close. He had left a small monitor hidden near the door and hadn't heard any sound. Ike would have alerted him to an intruder, but he didn't hear Sandy talk to the dogs either. Picking up his revolver, he quietly walked to his back porch. Sandy was sitting on her steps, looking out to the beach. He slid the weapon into the back of his jeans under his shirt, and walked out his porch door and over to where she sat.

"Restless?" he asked, and before she could answer, he said, "Let's take the dogs for a walk. They could use the exercise and so could I."

Without speaking, she took the hand he extended to her. She waited as he opened the porch door and removed the two leashes. The dogs ran down the steps and did their business, then waited for instructions. As he locked first her door and then his, he smiled.

"Hero is learning patience," he said.

"You've been working with him a lot," Sandy commented, as she reached down and ruffled the fur on the top of his head.

"He's smart, but stubborn, or it might be lazy. I haven't decided for sure," Longstreet said, as he clicked his fingers and both dogs walked near their owners. Ike walked close to his side. Hero's gait was more of a dance next to Sandy.

"He wants to run," Sandy said. "Why don't you run down the beach and back. I'll walk the same way and meet you further down."

Longstreet looked every direction. "I'll take them one at a time," he said. He put the brown leach on Hero and turned to Ike. "Alert!" he commanded. Then to Sandy, he said, "We'll be back soon."

Sandy watched them go. Hero was happy to be running next to his new friend as he jogged at a clip that exercised the dog without over exerting him. A couple times Longstreet looked back to make sure Ike was still obeying. Ike had matched his gait to Sandy's and walked right at her side. His head and ears told her he was watching and listening for trouble. He was really an amazing dog.

As Sandy watched Longstreet run, she remembered their relationship before she met Dasher; before Longstreet had moved to the mountains. She had believed there was something special between them then. He had kissed her a couple times, and since Dasher's death she had let herself remember those kisses. She had been remembering a lot of things about those days.

After fifteen minutes, Longstreet and Hero returned. She had never lost sight of them, but Hero was tired. He was happy when Sandy turned and they all walked back at a saunter.

Longstreet put the dogs on the porch.

"I'll be fine if you want to take Ike for a good run," she said.

"I'll take him tonight. Mike said he and Carla are bringing dinner."

"She called and insisted," Sandy said, "You'll join us, won't you?"

For the first time in a long time, Sandy saw Longstreet smile. "I'd love to," he said.

"Do you want to come in now?" she asked. "Dolley brought over a nice Cabernet yesterday. There's still half a bottle."

"I have some things to finish up at my place," he said. "What time are Mike and Carla coming over?"

"Carla said 5:00."

"I'll come by around 4:30," he said. "We can finish the bottle then."

"I'd like that," she smiled.

"See you then," he said, and walked back to his own porch.

Sandy went inside. She had time for a nice long soak in the tub and then she'd change into something nicer than her denim shorts and the soft, old, Galveston, Texas tee shirt that Carla had left behind.

Longstreet sat at his desk wondering if he was making a mistake by accepting her invitation. If he had his way, he'd be comforting her as he protected her, but he refused to allow himself that pleasure. She was a widow who had just lost her husband. He knew she was lonely, and she had seemed much too happy that he agreed. If a smile could put that old twinkle back in her eyes, he'd have to be very careful. Sandy was vulnerable now. The last thing he'd ever do was hurt her. He wondered if he had made a mistake walking away from her five years ago, but he had learned that looking back rarely benefits a person, so he didn't let his mind go there. He forced himself to finish the work on his desk. He'd take a shower and change clothes before dinner.

The front door opened at the Murrells Inlet office of Longstreet Campbell Investigations. Carla didn't recognize the good-looking man who entered.

She walked from her office to greet him.

"I'm here to see Will Carter," he said. "My name is Adam Chesterton."

Before Carla could respond, Will came from his office to the lobby. "Hey, Man, good to see you!" Will greeted.

"You look great," Adam said. "You really did become a lawyer."

"That was the reason for law school," Will smiled, as the two did a manly hug thing. "Carla, this is an old school buddy of mine. Adam, this is my boss, Carla Campbell, and that's her husband, Mike coming out of his office."

Mike walked over and shook hands with Adam, before draping his arm around Carla's shoulders. The three guys talked for a few minutes before Mike said, "I need my wife's help, so I'll let you guys visit."

"I'm treating Adam to Bovine's this evening," Will said. "Do you guys want to join us?"

"We're taking dinner to Sandy's," Mike said. "Appreciate the offer, though. Maybe next time you're in town."

"It's a plan," Adam said.

After Will and Adam reached Will's office, Mike said, "He seems like a nice guy."

"He does," Carla said, "Now what do you need me to find?"

"It's what I found that I want to show you," Mike smiled proudly.

Will closed his office door and directed Adam to the two leather Century Furniture chairs he had found in a consignment shop on Highway 17.

"Nice office," Adam smiled.

"Coffee, water, or something else?" Will asked.

"A water would be nice," Adam told him.

As Will pulled two waters from his small refrigerator, he asked his old friend, "Is this a personal visit or are you in need of an attorney?"

"Both," Adam said, "It's been too long since we talked, and I never got to express my condolences on you loosing Tammy. I always liked her. I followed your story and even read your book. You have been through a lot, man."

"It's history now," Will said, "but thanks. My mother wanted my story told, but it's hard to have it still current in the form of the book. I believe God took a hard situation and through it brought me here, but I choose to look forward these days. Reliving the past is just too hard."

"Well," Adam said, "I just wanted you to know I'm sorry for all you have gone through."

"Everyone has gone through something," Will said, sitting across from his old friend. "Tell me what's going on in your life."

"I'm married," Adam smiled, "and I have a baby son named Samuel. We call him Sammy."

"Samuel, after your father," Will said.

"Yes," Adam smiled. "My dad was killed the month before he was born."

"Killed?" Will repeated. "Why didn't I read that in the news?"

"It was officially reported as an accidental death," Adam told him. "My mother wanted it that way. The papers reported he had been in the wrong place at the wrong time and was merely another victim of a gang related shooting gone bad. I never believed that."

"You think someone targeted him?"

"I'm sure of it," Adam said. "He told me that day he was meeting a client in Mechanicsville, the toughest area on the south side of Atlanta. I wanted to go with him, but he said he'd be safe; he had his driver and it was daylight. They were meeting at a restaurant he had been to years before."

"Years?" Will asked.

"Exactly!" Adam said. "He was meeting an old college roommate in a place they used to go forty years earlier. I reminded him of Mechanicsville's reputation for violence, but he brushed it off as one more example of the media sensationalizing everything. That was our last conversation."

"Do you know the guy he was meeting?" Will asked.

"I only remember hearing his name, Gunthrie Williams. As far as I know, my father hadn't heard from him since college."

"Was he with your dad at the time of the shooting?"

"No, and I haven't been able to contact him," Adam said. "I'm not sure if he even arranged the meeting. My father might have been drawn there under false pretenses."

"What about his driver?" Will asked.

"They were both killed," Adam said.

"Sounds more targeted than random," Will agreed.

Adam took a drink of his water.

"What can I do?" Will asked.

"I've read about your investigation business," Adam said. "I don't want to go to someone in Atlanta, because I have a wife and baby to protect. If this was targeted, it may have something to do with the business of which I have now become the President."

Adam reached into his jacket pocket and produced a cell phone and a flash drive.

"I know this isn't your area of expertise, but it seems your office has people who know how to find information. This is my father's cell phone. The police asked about it, but I told them I had no knowledge of it."

"They can find information by just having the number," Will said.

"It's not his business phone," Adam told him. "It's one I found in my desk drawer the day he went to Mechanicsville. I have to believe he left it with me for a reason. I don't believe my father was into anything criminal, but until I know for sure, I wanted it to be in the possession of someone I could trust."

"Okay," Will said, taking the phone Adam handed him, "And the flash drive?"

"My mother gave me a tablet she found under the mattress when she was changing the sheets after my father died. She said she didn't have the password for it, but felt disloyal giving it to the police. She said at first she was going to get rid of it, but then decided to give it to me instead."

"Did you open it?" Will asked.

"Yes," Adam said, "I correctly guessed his password, but the information on it didn't mean anything to me. I copied everything on it to two flash drives and destroyed the tablet. No one else that I'm aware of even knows it existed."

"Is the information on it damaging?"

"I don't even know what any of it refers to," Adam shrugged.

"We have a forensic guy that can figure it out," Will said. "Did you suspect your father was into anything illegal or dangerous?"

"Never," Adam said, "but I've read enough spy novels to know anything is possible."

Will smiled. "You always did love those psychological thrillers. But I remember your father; he didn't seem the type to be lured into nefarious dealings."

"That's why it took me a while to come to you, but I want to know the truth," Adam said. "I need to know the truth. If there is something that could be harmful to my family or the company, I have to know what my father may have been involved in. We are a shipping company, after all. There is a lot of temptation to make big money by merely turning a blind eye and shipping unknown material in many forms. If it was happening, it still didn't mean my father had knowledge of it."

"Can you think of anyone whose manners or motives may seem questionable?" Will asked.

"No," Adam said, "I've looked at everyone involved in the company, but that's not my area of expertise."

Will laughed. "It wouldn't be. You're the most trusting and positive person I've ever been friends with. You never had a suspicious thought in your head."

"That was a more accurate appraisal before the shooting," Adam said. "Now, I feel like I suspect everyone. I need you to figure this out for me. I don't like not trusting people. It keeps me awake at night."

As Adam stood, Will did also.

"Bovine's tonight?" Will asked. "I'll pick you up at your hotel at 6:30?"

"That would be great," Adam said. "You can catch me up on your love life."

"That will be a short conversation, but I'm sure we'll find something to talk about. It's been many years since we had dinner together."

"And since we're not college age, we won't need to do shots," Adam laughed, as he patted Will's shoulder. "Those were never really your thing, but you'd always let me lead you down that path."

"I'm older and wiser now," Will smiled, "And looking forward to this evening."

"Me, too," Adam replied.

Chapter 10

Bella exited the bathroom at Bovine's. She had never met the attorney that worked with Carla, but she recognized him from his book jacket. He was in serious conversation with someone, so assuming it was attorney business she decided not to introduce herself tonight. There would be another time for that. His story intrigued her. Actually, her interest in him went beyond his story. Something about his eyes captivated her, and she had only seen them in pictures. She had imagined them looking so thoughtfully at her, but this didn't seem like the opportunity she was looking for. She would drop a hint to Reba that she'd like an introduction.

When she returned to the bar area, she was surprised to see two men seated at the table where she had left Reba sitting alone.

"Here she comes," the one man said and they both stood.

"You didn't tell me we had dates tonight," Bella said to Reba.

"We don't," Reba said, "These gentlemen were just leaving."

"Your friend doesn't seem to want our company," the man with the trimmed beard said. "We were hoping you would change her mind."

Bella walked around the men and leaned down to kiss a startled Reba who recovered quickly. "You aren't really our type," Bella said with a smile. Nodding to the two glasses on the table, she added, "But thank you for the drinks if you are responsible for those."

The men looked both surprised and amused. "I guess our gaydar is faulty this evening," the other one said. "Have a nice night, ladies."

"Bella," Reba laughed, once the men were out of earshot. "What if I had liked them?"

"Did you?" Bella asked.

"No," Reba said, "But we could have just said we weren't interested."

"They had already bought drinks. They wouldn't have taken a simple 'no thanks' without hanging around believing their charm would change our minds."

"You're probably right," Reba agreed, her attention back on the menu. "I think I'll have the Shrimp and Grits."

Bella sat, looked back at the menu and said, "I'm going for the Short Ribs. Should we trust the drinks we didn't order?"

"Now that you said that, I'm thinking not," Reba said. "Do you really think they would have spiked our drinks?"

"Who delivered them?"

"They walked over carrying them from the bar," Reba said.

"I think we stick with ordering our own drinks," Bella said. "We should take a sample to that cute forensic guy of Carla's and have him analyze it for drugs."

"We don't know their names and may never see them again," Reba said.

"Then I hope if they are spiked, some other more trusting girls don't get fooled by their charm," Bella said.

"They weren't that charming," Reba told her.

"There are some desperate girls out there," Bella reminded her. "But I guess we can't protect the ones we don't know. I'll have another drink when our server comes. How about you?"

"I'm still drinking this one," Reba said, "but I'll ask her to take the two new ones away."

"Should we tell her about Carla's forensic guy?" Bella asked.

"I think we should mind our own business," Reba laughed. "Maybe we're just two hot babes who attracted two nice guys and it's our loss."

"Maybe," Bella said, raising her glass to clink it against Reba's. "I like the hot babes image."

In the downstairs dining room, Will and Adam stayed away from anything connected to Tammy or Adam's father's murders.

"So, no girlfriend?" Adam asked, after they had ordered.

"No," Will said, "I was dating a girl for a while last summer, but it didn't become anything serious. I'm not even sure what I would want in a serious girlfriend or how I would cope in that arena. How did you meet your wife?"

"We met at a New Orleans trade show," Adam said. "She was a model at one of the big corporate booths. I watched her for a while, and then late that night she walked up and sat next to me at the bar. It had been a long day for each of us, and we were planning a nightcap before going to our respective rooms. She told the bartender she'd have what I was having, so I told him to put it on my tab. We started up conversation that lasted until the wee hours of the night at the bar. I was impressed and a bit smitten, but it didn't progress past smiles, laughs, and conversation. We both had early flights the next morning. I was flying back to Atlanta. She was flying back to Denver. We didn't exchange numbers, but we both would have been easy to find online."

"So, who called who?" Will asked.

"I wanted to call her, but my father was grooming me to take his place so he could retire. My mom had big retirement plans for them which were never realized. Anyway, I had little time for a relationship of any kind, let alone one with 1,400 miles between us."

"She called you," Will speculated.

"No. A driver for one of our long hauls had Covid, and the order had to be in Denver by Friday, so Dad tagged me to go. I had all this road time so I decided I'd give her a call. I figured she'd be too busy at the last minute for dinner after my delivery, but she said she was off on Saturday and suggested we meet for lunch. We had lunch together, dinner together, and talked by phone on much of my 21-hour drive home. I still hadn't kissed her, but I've since accused her of not kissing me on purpose. The anticipation of wrapping my arms around her and kissing her drove me crazy. We continued to talk often, and I finally invited her to spend the weekend before Christmas with me."

"You brought her home to meet the family?" Will asked.

"No way," Adam replied. "I told her Savanah, Georgia was beautiful at Christman and I'd book two rooms and pay for her flight if she'd agree to come. Seeing each other produced sparks. We were both thirty years old and knew what we wanted. We were married back in Savanah the following April, which resulted in Sammy being born on Super Bowl Sunday the fifth of February."

"Two rooms?" Will asked with one raised eyebrow.

Adam smiled sheepishly. "It started out as two rooms."

"So, knowing you, are you taking Sammy to Savanah this Christmas?" Will asked.

"No," Adam smiled, "We're leaving him with his grandparents and going back without him."

"Very romantic," Will said.

"It turns out I'm more romantic than even I knew," Adam said. "I guess it just takes the right girl."

"I'm happy for you," Will said.

"You'll meet someone one day that sweeps you off your feet," Adam said. "You already know marriage can be a good thing. Loving someone who loves you back is amazing. I still sometimes wonder how I got so lucky."

"Got a picture of your model wife?" Will asked.

Adam then showed Will a picture that exceeded his expectations. "She's gorgeous!" Will said.

"She's taken," Adam responded.

Will laughed. "I know, but wow!"

"She's as sweet as she is pretty," Adam said, then taking back his phone, he flipped to another picture. "And here's Samuel Adam."

"You named your kid after a beer?" Will said, "He'll grow up to hate you."

"No," Adam said. "He's named after his grandfather and his father. There is no 's' on Adam. Plus, he can go by Samuel A. Chesterton if he wants to. I'm okay with that. The next one can be named after Winny's family."

"Winny?"

"Winona Moore," Adam said. "Her father was Jackson Moore and her grandfathers were Franklin and Albert."

"I hope the second one isn't a girl," Will laughed.

"Oh, we'll argue over that name if it is," Adam smiled, "but in the end, whatever she wants will be fine with me."

Later, when Will dropped Adam off at his hotel, he told him he and Andrew would both look at what's on the flash drive and see if they could decipher anything useful. He also said they'd pull up the contacts and messages on the phone. As soon as they had anything, they'd let him know. The college roommates did a fist bump through the open driver's window as a camera with a long-range lens clicked off repeated shots.

Chapter 11

Mike and Carla ordered dinner from El Cerro Mexican Bar and Grill that was on their way home from work. Carla was pleased to see her mother dressed in a sharp grey and white striped shirtwaist tucked into a nice pair of fitted jeans with a wide black belt and multiple gold bracelets. Her hair and makeup were perfect. She looked like a younger Sandy, which meant she was beginning to care again.

Carla watched Longstreet for an indication that he noticed her mom's appearance, but if he did, he didn't let it show. Conversation was easy and pleasant during dinner. Afterwards, Mike made a second round of Margaritas, and suggested a game of Sequence—guys against the girls.

Carla realized they hadn't played any cards or games with her mother since before she married Dasher. Apparently, he didn't like cards or board games. Or maybe she hadn't suggested it when her mom was married to Dash. Carla would consider that later. As she set up the board on the porch, she heard her mother giving Longstreet a hard time about fearing he would lose.

"Lose to women?" he responded. "I don't think so. You forget Mike and I have tangled with terrorists."

"Who were men," Sandy said. "We're going to whip your butts tonight."

Carla entered the room to say, "Don't antagonize the bartenders. We trust them with mixing our drinks."

"Mike would never over-serve his mother-in-law," Sandy said.

"Was that a challenge?" Longstreet asked.

"She might be right," Mike said. "However, we've never seen Sandy inebriated. It might be fun."

"Oh, I love a rainy night," Longstreet began singing the old Eddie Rabbit song.

When Carla and Mike turned to Longstreet in surprise, they saw him wink at Sandy who blushed. Carla turned with a big smile to walk to the porch. Mike whispered in her ear, "That's interesting."

"I knew it," she whispered back to him.

"Knew what?" he said.

"We'll talk later," she smiled.

Longstreet and Sandy followed them to the porch where Carla had set up the game board, and put out small bowls of Pepitos, a snack food Mike liked to buy at a local Mexican market.

It didn't take long for the game to get rowdy, as four competitive players began talking smack and cheering on their partners.

The game ended with the guys winning at the last minute. The shout they gave was so loud it had both dogs on alert.

Longstreet laughed and told them to relax. Then he suggested they take the dogs for a walk on the beach. Carla said she and Mike were going to go.

"Vegas!" Longstreet challenged, "You lost your sense of romance? I remember when you and Mike couldn't get enough of that stuff."

"You've got to be kidding," Carla reacted to the taunt. "Mike and I have more game than you've ever had, old man!"

"Old man?" Longstreet responded, wrapping his arms around Sandy's waist and twirling her in a circle. "Let's walk the dogs," he said as he put her back on her feet.

"Is that a euphemism for something else?" Carla challenged.

"It means let's take the dogs for a walk," Longstreet replied. "There's a full moon on the beach, but if its past y'all's bedtime, we understand."

"I can assure you bedtime means more to us married folk than you pathetic singles," Carla replied. "Come on, Mike! We're going for a walk on the beach."

Mike looked at Sandy and said, "I think we should have cut those two off after the second Margarita."

The two couples and two dogs walked the beach in the moonlight. It was a perfect night on the ocean, as the pace of each couple settled down into a nice, quiet stroll.

"Why would anyone live anywhere else?" Sandy said, looking up at the moon and tripping on the uneven sand.

"Careful," Longstreet said, taking her hand to keep her from falling. As she regained her balance, he didn't let go.

Walking slowly, arm in arm behind Carla's mother, Longstreet, and the dogs, Mike said quietly, "What do you make of that?"

"I think it's about time," Carla said.

"You're kidding?" he replied.

"I'm not, but I'm still a little surprised."

"Do you think it's the tequila?"

"Only partially," she said.

Suddenly, Mike stopped, cupped Carla chin and kissed her hungrily. "I love the way your mind works," he said. "Let's turn and go home."

"Now," she smiled, "That's the tequila."

"Only partially," he responded, putting his finger before his lips in a shh manner, he took her hand and they turned and began running back toward the house. Carla tried not to trip or laugh, as they thought it was so funny to be ditching Sandy and Longstreet.

They got back to Sandy's house, got in their car and Mike started the engine.

"How long do you think it will take them to know we aren't behind them anymore?" he asked.

"I don't know," she responded, "but I'm not sure they care."

"And that doesn't surprise you?" he asked.

"We'll see if it translates into tomorrow," Carla said. "Your friend is a complicated guy."

"And your mother isn't?" Mike said.

"Isn't what?" Carla asked.

"Complicated," he replied.

"You like complicated," she said, reaching over and taking his hand as he drove the short drive to their home.

"Only in you," he said, squeezing her hand. "I like the rest of the world to be easy."

"That's bull," she said, "a special-forces guy never goes for the easy."

"That guy is history," Mike said.

"Not to me, he isn't," she smiled. "I married a man who is willing to take on anyone for truth and justice. He thrives on complicated."

"Only partially," he repeated.

"So, when we get home, do you want easy or complicated?" she teased.

"When he didn't respond, she said, "Mike, did you go to sleep?"

"No," he said, "I'm imaging easy and complicated in my mind."

"And which did you decide?" she asked.

"I'm thinking I'd like a little of each," he said.

"And I'm thinking I'll surprise you," she added.

"And I'm thinking I've got the best wife in the world," he said.

"And I'm thinking you've got that right."

Stretching both arms over her head, Carla said, "But I think that tequila is making me sleepy."

Mike pushed his foot down on the accelerator, and Carla laughed.

Chapter 12

The following day, Carla had an early morning business phone call. Around 10:30, she had a break at work and called her mother, hoping for an update as to how her evening ended.

"Are you alone?" Carla asked Sandy.

"I'm never alone anymore," Sandy said.

"Is that a bad thing?" Carla asked.

"I would like my old life back," she responded.

"Which old life?"

"What is that supposed to mean?" Sandy snapped.

"Did I call at a bad time?" Carla asked cautiously.

"And what is that supposed to mean?"

"Listen, I'm not sure what to say right now, so why don't you call me back when you feel like talking," Carla said.

"I'm sorry," Sandy responded. "I haven't had a hangover since I don't know when. Yes, I do. It was before you came back from Texas. I'm a little edgy this morning."

"Okay," Carla said. "Want me to pick you up for lunch? I'll see if Dolley wants to meet us at Taproom. A bowl of Russ's soup with some dry crackers might help."

"No, I think I'll go back to bed," Sandy said. "I don't think I'd be very good company today."

"Take a nap," Carla said. "I have some work to do. Dolley or I will pick you up at 1:00, and the three of us will have a simple Taproom lunch."

"I don't know," Sandy sighed.

"Take some aspirin with a glass of tomato juice and go back to bed. One of us will pick you up. It's just Taproom. You can wear a hat and dark glasses if you want."

"Very funny," her mother said. "You win. I'll see you later."

Dolley picked Sandy up at the scheduled time. Sandy wore a pair of gauzy navy pants, a loose cotton top, a baseball cap and sunglasses. Longstreet walked out from his house to greet Dolley and take the dogs back home with him.

"You girls just going to Taproom?" he asked.

"I didn't tell you we were going there," Sandy said.

"Mac did," Longstreet told her. "I'll take the boys for a run on the beach while you're gone."

"Do whatever you want," Sandy said, before turning and getting in Dolley's car.

"Wow," Dolley said, as she backed out of the driveway. "That wasn't a very sweet goodbye. What's going on?"

"Nothing. Absolutely nothing," Sandy stated.

The traffic light turned red as Dolley approached Atlantic Avenue. As they idled at the intersection, she asked, "Am I then correct in thinking you wish something was going on?"

"Carla and Mike brought dinner last night and I drank too much," she answered. "Why is everyone making a federal case out of it."

"You snapped at Longstreet and I just asked what was going on," Dolley said.

"I'm just tired of being babysat," Sandy said. She decided not to repeat what she told Carla that she wanted her old life back.

"Longstreet?" Dolley said asked.

"I can't figure him out," Sandy sighed. "It's like 90% of the time he acts like being with me is a job he'd rather not have, but then every so often a little bit of that guy I was attracted to comes through—just enough to throw me off balance."

"He had dinner with ya'll last night?" Dolley guessed.

"Yes. He was funny and even a little flirty. Carla and Mike wanted to go for a walk on the beach after the guys beat us at Sequence. At one point I tripped. Longstreet caught me and took my hand. Then he didn't let go as we continued walking. We had the dogs with us, so we didn't talk much, but it was nice. When I turned around to talk to Carla and Mike, they were gone. We walked back slowly with the dogs, and I was remembering the old days. I recounted an old memory to him and we both laughed."

"So, why are you upset with him?"

"When we got back to the house, he said goodnight on the porch, and told me to go on to bed, saying he had to get something from his house. I changed into my pajamas and robe and waited for him to return. After I finally turned out the lights and went to bed, I heard him come in to sleep on the sofa."

"You were hoping for a romantic evening?" Dolley asked.

"No, not exactly," Sandy responded. "I just wanted to sit up and talk, but he purposefully went to his house until he knew I was in bed. It was obvious he was tired of my company."

Dolley merely smiled as the light turned green and she pulled onto Atlantic Avenue.

"Why the smirk?" Sandy asked.

"That wasn't a smirk; it was a smile," Dolley told her. "You had too much to drink, put on your pajamas and waited for him to come back. Sandy Asher, the seductress, didn't get a chance to show the stoic Allen Longstreet her sexy side."

"That's not it," Sandy argued. "He was being sweet. I just wanted to continue talking with him. It was like the old days. We used to be able to talk about anything, more than Dash and I did. I miss that."

"Maybe he knew you had too much to drink and was being a gentleman," Dolley said. "You know, like in the old romantic movies."

"I wasn't trying to seduce him," Sandy stated. "I wanted to sit up and talk. I thought last night we had a little of our old connection back, but I guess I just misread the situation."

"I'm sorry," Dolley said. "I'm sure part of it is that you miss Dasher. Don't be so hard on yourself. You are grieving and lonely and men can be clueless. Longstreet isn't heartless. He probably thought giving you some space was the right thing to do."

"Maybe," was all Sandy answered.

They met Carla at Taproom and hadn't been there long when Elsa stopped by with Devon and Astrid. Devon raced to his father who gave him a Maraschino cherry from behind the bar. Then he saw his mom was talking to Dolley, so he ran to join them.

"Miss Dolley," Devon squealed.

"Hi, Darlin'," she smiled. "Come sit by me."

Devon crawled up onto the bench and looked to see what Dolley was eating.

"You hungry?" she asked, and laughed when he nodded.

"Devon," Elsa scolded, "we just had lunch at home. Don't be a beggar. It isn't polite."

Dolley ignored Elsa and moved her plate toward Devon, offering him her French fries.

"He's like a bottomless pit these days," Elsa sighed.

"Miss Dolley?" Devon said.

"Gentlemen don't talk with food in their mouth," Dolley told him.

Devon dutifully chewed as Elsa started a conversation with Sandy about Rose's upcoming birthday. As soon as he swallowed, he asked, "When can we come to your pool again? You have the very best pool at a house. The one at Wahoo Park is bigger, but it has big kids. One knocked me down, but my mom said it was an accident."

"I'm sure she was right," Dolley told him. "Who would knock down a cute little kid like you?"

"I'm not little," he told her. "Astrid is little. I'm the big brother and I have to act like it my dad says."

"I think that is good advice," Dolley smiled. "She will always look up to you if you do."

"What are you drinking?" he asked.

"Devon," Elsa said, "You are not drinking Miss Dolley's drink. We just stopped to give something to your dad, so get down and let's go. If you're thirsty, your dad will give you some water."

"Good-bye, Miss Dolley," he said. "I have to go now."

"Have a good day," she replied, as he slid off the bench.

"I will," he called as he ran to his father at the bar.

"I remember when I couldn't wait for him to walk," Elsa sighed. "He somehow skipped that step and went from crawling to running." With her daughter on her hip, she followed her son to the bar.

Sandy seemed to have perked up over lunch. When she excused herself to go to the bathroom, Carla said, "Longstreet joined us for dinner at Mom's last night."

"That's what I heard," Dolley said.

"Did she tell you how the evening ended?" Carla wanted to know. "I asked her and she wasn't willing to talk about it."

"It seems he excused himself to do something at his house, and didn't return to hers until after she turned out the lights and went to bed."

"Really," Carla said. "They seemed to be getting along when Mike and I left them on the beach."

"She said that also," Dolley confided. "It is all so hard for her right now."

"But her faith always carried her through the tough times," Carla said.

"It will again," Dolley assured Carla. "She's older and this time was different. I'm sure there is guilt she didn't have with the others."

"How was she responsible?" Carla asked.

"If Dash hadn't married her, he'd still be alive."

"That's ridiculous," Carla stated. "You could say that about a lot of situations, that doesn't make what happen your fault."

"I know that, and at some level, so does she," Dolley said. "It's part of her grief process this time and she expected Longstreet to be more of a confidant."

"What do you mean?"

"I think she'd like him to be more consoling and he's staying very reserve around her."

"He wasn't reserve last night," Carla said.

"And that confuses her," Dolley said as Sandy approached the table.

Lunch continued with happy conversation. Carla offered to see what Rose would like to do for her birthday. As always, Dolley said her house was an option.

When Carla got back to work, Andrew had information for her. The police had more information on the man who killed Dr. Asher.

"It seems the man who killed the doctor was a nobody," he told her. "By showing his picture around, they located the hotel where he was staying. There they found a fake ID with a Miami address. He had rented a car at the Miami Airport and driven to Myrtle Beach according to the mileage on the rental agreement found in his car parked in a lot at the Myrtle Beach Airport."

"Nothing at the hotel told them anything?" Sandy asked.

"There was an empty envelope in his travel bag containing only the killer's fingerprints. The ID he checked in with said his name was John Lopez, age 32. The desk clerk described tattoos that led investigators to a street gang in Miami by the name of Baby Demons. The only connection the Miami cops uncovered was a girlfriend that said John had come into some money, a supposed inheritance from his abuelo, and he left town for a family reunion. She was worried because she hadn't been able to reach him since the night of the murder. No gang members were able to identify his picture, but that was as expected."

"So, we have nothing," Sandy said.

"The money indicates he was paid to do the job," Andrew said. "Whoever chose him didn't want a professional who might be traced back to him or her. He was probably a thug who had killed as part of a gang initiation. The cops said his girlfriend was adamant that he wasn't a violent guy. Before he left Miami, he'd bought her an engagement ring."

"So, he'll probably show up in her life again?" Carla surmised.

"That's what the police think. They're keeping an eye on her place."

"If she alerts him, he won't come back," she said.

"He could send for her," Andrew said, "or the ring was just a payment for past services rendered."

"You're a cynic," she said.

"Just looking at all the options," he replied. "If it was true love, as you'd like to believe, he'll contact her when he thinks it is safe. If not, depending on the amount of money he received, he could be gone."

"On foot?" she asked.

"He might have another ID, and he might have changed appearances to either rent a new car or fly somewhere else."

"So, he could be gone," she stated.

"Unless it was love," Andrew smiled. "We can only hope."

Carla went back to her office. She didn't want this guy to get away.

Chapter 13

Reba was bored. She had invited Will for dinner and had decided to make one of her mother's few gourmet recipes, Porchetta Pork Chops. She went to Fresh Market for the pork chops and fresh rosemary. Exiting her car, she decided to walk through Chico's and maybe find a new book to read at Litchfield Books next door.

After trying on various jeans and tops combinations, she bought a pair of embellished black jeans and a rather tight-fitting gold top. She had a black necklace at home that would finish the outfit. Leaving Chico's, she walked to the book store. Upon entering, she spotted Bella.

"Hey, neighbor," she said. "Find any good reading material?"

"Reba," Bella exclaimed, "I haven't seen you this week. Were you out of town?"

"Just doing research for a new book idea," Reba said. "When I'm focused on a project, I become a hermit."

"I wish that was my problem," Bella said. "I came in here to read book jackets, still hoping for the inspiration that would send me down a writing path."

"No luck?" she asked. "Starting to doubt God's intervention into your career path?"

"I'm doubting me, not God," Bella responded.

"I'm not sure how you can separate that in your case," Reba said. "You are only pursuing this course because you believe in your grandmother's visions."

Bella sighed. "The lack is in me, not my grandmother or God," she said.

"Whatever," Reba said. "I'm looking for a good book. Have any of those jacket covers you read sounded good?"

"Have you read this author?" Bella asked. "He's from around her and his mysteries have a dark side."

Reba picked up the book and read the back cover. "I'm not really into fantasy," she said, replacing the book. "Maybe something with a historical flavor."

"For inspiration?" Bella asked.

"No, more of a distraction," Reba told her. "When I need a break in what I'm writing, I chose something completely different to read. It helps me somehow."

"I'm still trying to figure all this out," Bella said. "I see you stopped at Chico's."

"I invited Will for dinner tonight and on my way to the Market for pork chops, I decided to get a new outfit and a book."

"Will, the attorney that works for Carla?" Bella asked. "I didn't know you two were an item."

"We aren't," she answered. "Just friends, although he is pretty cute. A girl could do worse. I think I'll peruse the historical novels so I can get to the market and back home. Let's have coffee or a glass of wine this week."

"I'd like that," Bella said, turning back to the book in her hand.

Reba bought a book by an author she knew and waved at Bella as she left the bookstore. Once home, she put the thick, boneless pork chops in apple juice and salt brine to soak, while she chopped veggies for a salad and made sure she had everything ready for the caramelized onion risotto she was planning as her side. Dinner would take around an hour and a half to prepare, so she decided to go ahead and fix her hair and get dressed early.

Will arrived promptly at 6:00, dressed in a polo shirt and khaki slacks, carrying a bottle of Chardonay. Reba greeted him and thanked him for the wine.

"Something smells really good," he said.

"Hopefully it tastes as good as it smells," Reba smiled. "Come into the kitchen. You can open and pour your wine while I finish dinner."

Conversation was easy as they sat in the kitchen while Reba slid the pork chops and finished the Risotto. As the two dishes were ready, she tossed the salad with dressing. They were just starting to eat when there was a knock on the door. Reba was surprised when, before she could get up, the door opened and Bella entered with a vase of flowers.

"Reba said she had a dinner guest," she said, walking to the table where Reba and Will sat. "I didn't mean to interrupt your meal. I just thought I'd bring something to add to her evening, but I see you already thought of fresh flowers on your table. I'm Bella," she added, extending a hand to Will.

"I'm Will," he smiled, shaking her hand.

Reba stood and took the flowers from Bella. "That was nice of you," Reba said, "I'm sorry I only made two pork chops."

"Oh, I'd never think of interrupting your dinner," Bella said. "I'm pleased to meet you Will. Are you the Will that works with Carla?"

"Guilty," he smiled, his eyes displaying a slight twinkle.

"Well, I've heard good things," Bella said. "I'll let you go back to your lovely dinner. It smells wonderful."

Bella smiled at Reba and left.

"Well," she said after the front door closed. "That was unexpected."

"Did she mean well?" he asked.

"I'm sure she did," Reba laughed, "but it could make a good beginning to a mystery book."

Will gave a little laugh and resumed eating. Bella was not mentioned again.

Next door, Bella was soon curled up in her long navy-blue negligee with the futuristic fantasy she had picked out to read. As she shifted to reach for her cup of tea, the soft fabric brushed across her skin, causing her to sigh. Will Carter was as exciting in person as she had imagined. His eyes were captivating, even in the few seconds that he smiled at her. She had hoped Reba might invite her to stay, but that hadn't happened. So, she had delivered her flowers, introduced herself and left. It had been a bold move, but she believed she had pulled it off without embarrassing herself. She just needed to meet him in person. The man on the book jacket turned out to be all she had imaged him to be. Now she could stop by Carla's and poke her head into his office to say hello. That would be the natural result of this evening. Bella was pleased with herself as she sipped her tea. Her Grandmother

Lettie was coming next week. Bella needed her to meet Will and assess if there might be a chance God saw them together in the future.

Longstreet was on his computer when he was alerted by a single bark followed by a growl from Ike. Hero now joined in with incessant barking. Longstreet picked up his weapon and looked from his back door toward Sandy's. He relaxed as he realized Ike had alerted him to a pizza delivery boy who was about to leave with the pizza.

"Relax!" Longstreet called to both the boy and the dog. As Ike relaxed, the boy turned toward him and said, "That's one scary dog, Mister."

"He's supposed to be," Longstreet smiled. "I'm sorry he scared you."

"I'm supposed to deliver a pizza to that address," he replied, as Sandy walked onto the porch.

Longstreet walked out his porch door and took the pizza from the kid. "Is it paid for?" he asked.

"No, Sir," the boy said, "It's $23.50."

Longstreet reached into his pocket and pulled out three ten-dollar bills. "Here ya go," he said. "I'll deliver it to the lady."

"Thanks," the boy said, handing him the box and heading toward his car. "That's one scary dog," he repeated.

Longstreet walked toward where Sandy was watching the exchange. He smiled at her and asked, "Wanna share? I haven't eaten all day."

Sandy didn't reply, but opened her door and waited for him to climb the steps to enter.

"I haven't seen you in a few days," she said, as he walked past her to the kitchen.

"I sleep here every night," he said.

"And yet I haven't seen you," she repeated. "I'm surprised you want to share a pizza since I've had the feeling you're avoiding me since our walk on the beach."

Longstreet didn't reply, but merely put the pizza box on the counter and opened the lid. "Looks good," he said.

"If you're going to stay, can we talk?" she asked.

"Do you have anything to go with this pizza?" he asked.

"Like salad or drink?" she asked.

"I was thinking a wine or a beer," he said.

"Both," she replied, "but you didn't answer my question."

"I'm staying," he said, going to the refrigerator and pulling out a beer. "Can I get one for you, too?" he asked.

When she nodded, he handed her the one in his hand and reached for another. Sandy took the beer, and pulled two tall glasses from the cabinet. She also pulled out two plates and two cloth napkins. Longstreet poured the beers, as Sandy retrieved a spatula from the drawer. She put two pieces of pizza on a plate that she handed Longstreet.

"Where to?" he asked, beer in one hand, plate and napkin in the other.

"Let's eat on the porch," she said. "It's a nice evening."

With plate, napkin and glass in hand, Sandy followed her guest to the back porch. There was a breeze off the water tonight, and the lapping of the waves was a soothing sound. Ike was on his blanket. Hero was at Sandy's side, hoping for a handout. No one spoke at first.

"I'm sure Carla told you they know who shot Dasher," he said.

"She did," Sandy responded, "but they seem to have little information to find him."

"The theory is he wasn't after you or Dash," Longstreet said. "For that reason, he may be afraid to surface."

"What do you mean?" she asked. "Carla said he has a fiancé in Florida."

"He does," Longstreet said, "but he also accepted money for a hit and blew his target. Whoever paid him will not want him caught and questioned by the police and he knows it. He may not love his girl as much as he loves his life."

"So, we may never know?" Sandy said.

"Just because he doesn't want to be found, doesn't mean we won't eventually find him. We have his fingerprints from the hotel and we know what he looked like from his fake ID."

"He could change his appearance," Sandy said.

"He probably already has," he agreed, "but running and hiding is not as easy as it sounds. He may get away, but he may not. We'll see how creative he is. A lot of people have his face to watch for."

"How long are you stuck babysitting me?" she asked, abruptly changing the conversation.

"Stuck babysitting you?" he replied, setting his pizza on the side table and leaning back with his beer in his hand.

"It's obviously not something you want to do," she said, stiffly not looking his way.

"Sandy," he said her name quietly and waited for her to look his direction. When she did, he continued. "I know this is a very hard time for you. I'm trying not to make it harder."

"By ignoring me?" she accused. "By not talking to me or even wanting to let me talk? Is that how you were taught at the academy to treat a victim or a hostage?"

"A hostage?" he asked.

"That's how this feels," she said, as a tear slid down her cheek. "We used to be friends, Allen. Now, I'm nothing more than a distasteful job to you. I don't understand why. Five years ago, I didn't walk away from you. You left me."

"You were happy with Dash," he said. "He could offer you so much more than I ever could."

"Like what?" she wanted to know.

"Sandy," he hesitated, and then continued. "I've only had one relationship in my life and I was terrible at it. I don't know how to be soft and tender."

"That's a lie and an excuse," she said, angrily. "You've been tenderhearted toward me in the past, but something's changed that I don't understand. You show more affection to Hero than you do to me. I'm not asking you to want me, but at least you could want to sit with me."

"We've been together day and night for weeks," he said.

"No," she responded, "We sat together after the murder, but lately you only sleep here. Even when you were here during the day, you didn't want me talking to you unless I had a memory that would help the case."

"That's not true," he argued.

"But it is," she said.

"You had just lost your husband in a violent way," he told her. "I was trying to facilitate your situation with an understanding for your loss and grief."

"Facilitate my situation," she said, emphasizing each word. "That's very noble of you, Agent Longstreet, but I would have much more appreciated your friendship. Allen, we used to be friends."

"We still are," he said, quietly.

"Only a couple moments in several weeks did it feel that way," she replied.

Allen knew exactly which moments she was referring to. He wasn't sure how to respond. It would be unprofessional to develop a relationship with her at this point as she was still recovering from the shock of a trauma and the loss of her husband. As sincere as she sounded, he understood her vulnerability more than she did. It was not a time to share his feelings or regrets. As he debated on how to respond, he realized his response was taking too long.

"I'm not sure what to say," he said, feeling clumsy and knowing whatever he said would be inadequate.

"I see," she said, setting the glass she had been holding, but never drank from on the side table. "I don't think the pizza settled well in my stomach," she said as she stood. "I'm going to go to bed. You can take the pizza back to your place if you want. After all, you did pay for it."

Allen watched as she sadly walked back into her house. He knew he should have said something, anything, but he didn't want to mess this up. As the door to her bedroom closed, he realized he had done just that. He carried the two glasses back to the kitchen and poured the untouched one down the drain. He then cleaned up, throwing away her partially eaten pizza and wrapping the rest for the refrigerator. He took the dogs out, locked up his house, and returned to Sandy's sofa. He found an old black and white mystery on the television and turned the volume down low. He'd be here if she decided to join him, but he didn't expect that she would. As he ate his pizza and drank his beer, he realized that was the first thing he'd been right about all evening. It was hours before he turned off the TV and attempted to fall sleep.

Chapter 14

Carla was on her computer with Will leaning over her shoulder when Bella walked in.

"I didn't hear you come in," Carla said, surprised and disturbed that someone entered without her knowledge.

"Your lab guy, Dr. Bennett held the door for me," she said. "Was I supposed to announce myself? Is there a password?"

Carla smiled. "No, come on in," she said. Will had stood up and Carla introduced them.

"We met at Reba's recently," Will said.

"I was hoping we could have lunch together," Bella said, "I still only know a few people here." She shrugged her shoulders and waited.

"I'd love to," Carla said, "but Mike and I are meeting Detective Baker in Myrtle Beach in a little bit."

"What about you, Will?" Bella asked. "Interested in a free lunch? I'm buying."

"I'll go as long as you let me buy," he answered with a smile. "My upbringing wouldn't allow me to let a lady buy lunch."

"We can go Dutch then," she said.

"We'll see," he said, as he walked with her out of Carla's office. "I have to email one thing to Carla and then we can leave."

Bella watched him walk to his office as Carla walked out of hers.

"Very smooth," Carla said.

"I actually came to have lunch with you," Bella told her.

"He's a good substitute," Carla said.

"Seems like a nice guy," Bella added, nonchalantly.

"And kind of hot," Carla said.

"Really," Bella smiled. "I hadn't noticed."

"Then you're blind," Carla replied.

"Ready?" Will said as he walked toward the two women.

"I am," Bella said, and winked at Carla behind Will's back.

Carla wasn't sure how she felt about that possible relationship, but it wasn't her business. She returned to her office to open the email Will had just sent.

Bella let Will drive and pick the restaurant. He pulled up in front of J. Peters Bar and Grill on the Marsh Walk. It wasn't as quiet or romantic as some places might have been, but it wasn't like a date. It was lunch.

They were able to get a table outside with a view of the marsh and the people walking by. The table next to them had two boisterous, young boys wanting the attention of their mother who was on her phone.

Shortly after they ordered iced teas and sandwiches, a soft Nerf-style ball hit the side of Will's face and landed on their table. A cute boy from the next table appeared to apologize and ask for his ball back.

"What's your name?" Will asked.

"Billy," he said. "I'm going to be a Chief when I grow up."

"An Indian chief?" Will asked.

"No," Billy told him, "A Kansas City Chief."

"Are you from Kansas City?"

"Never been there, but my dad promised when I'm big enough, he'll take me to a game."

"Then why do you want to play for that team?" Will asked.

"Because they're the best, and I want to be the best."

"Why?" Will asked.

"Why not?" Billy said, taking his ball and going back to his table.

"I'm thinking there might be big things in that boy's future," Will chuckled.

"Did you and your wife want children?" Bella asked.

"You know my story," Will stated.

"I've read your book," Bella said, "I'm sorry for your losses."

"It's a history book," he said, "I've moved on."

"I didn't mean anything by mentioning your past," Bella said apologetically.

"Don't worry about it," he said. "Reba told me you moved here to become a writer."

"You guys were talking about me?" she smiled coyly.

"Not really," he hastened to say, "She just mentioned that she hadn't known you long and you came to the beach to write as she had."

"Not exactly the same," Bella said, "but similar. I'm afraid my quest isn't going as smoothly as hers did. It was more my grandmother's idea for me to be here. I was actually happy living on her ranch in Colorado."

"I've never been to Colorado," Will said, "but that location keeps coming up in my research these days."

"How so?" she asked.

"Just keep coming across people from there, not so much anything about the state. Did your grandparents have a large ranch?"

"They did," she said, and proceeded to tell him about her horses and her life before moving to Murrells Inlet.

As the server cleared their plates and Will asked for the check, Bella said, "I have been watching the weather this week. You've lived on the coast for a while. Does the threat of a hurricane make you nervous?"

"Not nervous, but cautious," he said.

"What does that mean?" she wanted to know.

"I have great respect for weather," he said.

"You mean like climate change?"

"No. Maybe I should say my respect is for the forces that God put into creation."

"You mean God causes natural disasters?"

"Not that either," Will said as he put cash in the folder to pay the bill and tip the server.

Will smiled as they both rose from their chairs. He looked at his watch and said, "I have time to walk the boardwalk out into the marsh if you want. It's a pretty day and I'll probably be in the office late tonight."

He started to put his hand on her back to guide her through the others leaving at the same time, but thought it might be inappropriate. Sometimes he wasn't sure what proper etiquette looked like these days.

After they passed The Claw House, the foot traffic became lighter, so he resumed their previous conversation.

"I don't know where you stand in your faith in God," he said, "but my faith in him is strong. I have discovered what God is like by studying my Bible. Since you read my story, you know I had nearly a year with plenty of time to read."

Bella didn't respond, so he continued. "God created a perfect world before he created man and woman. He gave them everything with only one rule. When they broke that rule, everything changed, and Satan gained control of more than God had originally designed. It was the natural consequence of what we know as the fall of man."

"So, you're saying natural disasters are the work of Satan?" she asked, skeptically. "I thought God was in control of everything."

"It's tricky," Will told her. "I believe God is not in control like a puppet master, because he gave man free will. He is the top authority like the CEO for a company, which means he doesn't control the day-by-day activities or the minute-by-minute decisions of his employees and staff."

"So, who do you believe is control of the weather?"

"I believe that the weather is the result of natural occurrences such as wind streams and heat indexes and atmospheric pressures," he said.

"Then where does Satan figure into weather?" she asked.

"That's another thing I determined in my studies," he told her as they slowly walked past the marina, heading along the wooden walkway over the marsh. "If you go back and read Genesis 1, it says God made light and vegetation and creatures, and called them all good."

"Okay," she encouraged, fascinated by his words.

"If you re-read verse 2 where God created the atmosphere or what we call the sky, God does not call that good," Will told her.

"He doesn't? I didn't know that," she said.

"I believe God gave dominion or rule to man over everything in this world except for the atmosphere. I believe that's Satan's realm, and of that he has control. He has many names in the Bible. In Ephesians 2:2, Satan is called the Prince of the power of the air."

"You mean there he has control over God?" she asked.

"Of course not, but like a CEO and those VP's he puts in charge of the many facets of his company, for now God has stepped back giving man dominion over the earth, of which we have not always taken good care, and Satan has dominion over the atmosphere. One day we know Satan will lose everything he has tried to acquire of God's, but for now the skies belong to him. At least, that's how it appears to me."

"Wow," she said, "You have really thought this through. My father and my grandmother taught me to read my Bible so that I would understand what Jesus meant when he said he was the only way to God, but I never dug into questioning things as you must have."

Will smiled. "I had a lot of time on my hands, remember?"

"Is your prison time one of those things like when the Bible says man meant it for evil, but God works all things for good?"

Again, Will smiled.

"What?" she asked.

"I think you just blended the words of Joseph and Paul, but yes. I believe I came out of prison a better man than the one I was when I went in."

They walked for a while in comfortable silence.

"So, what did you mean hurricanes make you cautious, not nervous?"

"You really listen," he observed.

"Only to smart people that I respect," she smiled.

"I appreciate the compliment," Will said. "I guess when it comes to hurricanes, I think of them as a part of living by the ocean. If you live in the Midwest, you respect tornado warnings. If you live in the far north, you respect sub-zero temperatures. I guess what I'm saying is that I don't fear hurricanes, but I respect the fact that they can be deadly. If the weather channel says one is massive and heading toward where I live, I would obey the order to evacuate, but I don't run to the middle of the state for every tropical storm."

"That makes sense," she said. "I'm glad we had lunch today."

"Me, too," Will said.

They talked about a couple signs they passed as they walked back toward where Will parked, and the fact that it was low tide.

"Being born in a Mexico pueblo, growing up in the Rocky Mountains, going to college in Arkansas, and now living here," Bella said, "I've experienced so many different climates. Here people discuss the tides; in the mountains people talked about Chinook Winds."

"I never heard of them," Will said.

"You would if you lived in the Rockies," Bella told him. "They are an unnaturally dry wind that can melt snow, cause erosion, and often reduce the amount of food available for wildlife and herds."

"What causes them?" he asked.

"It's when there is a downslope of wind that is unusually warm and dry. They happen on the east side of the mountains, and are even said to cause headaches, irritability, anxiety and dry skin."

"Wow," Will exclaimed, "that's very interesting. Will you write about a Chinook in one of your books?"

Bella laughed. "So far, I have no books except in the mind of my Grandmother Lettie."

"Do you want to write a book?" Will asked.

"I'm not sure anyone has asked me that quite so bluntly," she stated.

"I'm sorry," Will said. "I didn't mean to be rude."

"No, don't apologize. If I'm honest, the answer is no, but I have been taught to be open to what God wants from me; you know, to respect what is his plan for my life."

"I have a theory on that, too," Will said, "but I'll save it for another time."

They crossed the parking lot to his car, where he unlocked and opened the passenger door for her, and closed it when she was in.

On the way back to the office she asked why he'd be working late tonight. Again, he was surprised at how closely she listened to his words. He explained he was working on a legal case that required him to know more than he did about a certain industry, so he had a lot of reading to do.

"Since I have no real reason to go home," he said, "I'm in the habit of staying at the office when there is a pressing issue."

"I can understand that," she stated.

When they got back to the office, Bella thanked him for her lunch, and he thanked her for having the idea for lunch. He watched her walk toward her car, thinking she was an interesting person. She was having the same thought about him.

Chapter 15

Monday morning, Dolley decided to cancel her weekend invitation for everyone to celebrate Rose's birthday at her house due to the threat of a hurricane coming up the east coast of Florida. It made landfall in Homestead, Florida, south of Miami, as a tropical depression, but as it remained at sea it had been upgraded to a possible hurricane due to its slow progress. It was picking up water, with anticipated high wind speeds if it turned back west along the South Carolina coast. People living near the beach were boarding up their homes, evacuating, or both. Tap helped Chip board up the house on the marsh that had belonged to Rose's grandparents.

"I can see why she loves this place," Tap said. "It's beautiful and peaceful here."

"It is beautiful, but if a storm hits at or right before high tide, it could take in water," Chip said, "although, according to Rose, it never has. It seems this little section of land was built up high enough that the water flows around it."

"So, you could get stuck here," Tap said.

"Temporarily, I suppose," Chip replied.

"You're welcome to stay at the apartment over the restaurant next weekend if you don't want to drive across the state."

"We've been talking about making a trip to the mountains. This seemed like a good time to go," Chip said. "That's why I wanted to get these windows boarded so we could leave tomorrow and avoid any exiting traffic if it looks like the South Strand is in for a direct hit."

"We've been promising Olivia we'd come to visit her and DJ at Quantico," Tap said. "We might try a road trip next month. A day in the car sounds a bit daunting to me with a baby and a toddler."

"We've never gone further than Charleston with Daisy," Chip stated, "but she seems to be a good traveler. I guess if we take that trip we'll know."

"I'm sure Astrid will fare better than Devon. Quantico is at least six and a half hours. That's a long time for Devon to sit still," Tap said.

"Maybe try a little Dramamine," Chip suggested.

"You mean drug him?" Tap asked, not sure if Chip was serious.

"I wouldn't think of it that way," Chip said. "I'm sure they have something for children who get motion sickness that makes them drowsy."

"I'm not sure Elsa would approve," Tap said.

"Just a thought," Chip said. "If the trip north is bad, you still have to make the trip again to get home."

Tapp didn't respond, but Chip could tell his idea might not sound as crazy as Tap originally thought.

That evening in Pawley's Island, Reba was typing on her computer, when her doorbell rang. Answering the door, she found Bella wearing a big smile and with holding up a bag.

"What's that?" Reba asked, opening the door wider so Bella could enter.

"An unassembled charcuterie board if you're free this evening."

"Where is it going?" Reba asked.

"What?"

"Where are you taking the charcuterie board after we assemble it?" Reba asked again, as Bella and the shopping bag headed toward Reba's kitchen island.

"I brought it for us to eat," Bella said. "I was going to assemble it at my place, but decided I'd rather do it with you. Are you busy?"

"I was writing, but I need to stop. I'd love for you to stay, but Marti is coming over later. Will that be a problem?" Reba asked.

"Not for me," Bella said, "And I have plenty of food in this bag. Will she mind if I'm here?"

"No, we just haven't seen each other lately and she called to see if I wanted to grab a bite to eat. Let's see what you have in that bag."

The two women were just putting the finishing touches on a pretty impressive charcuterie board when Reba's front door opened and Marti called, "Hello!"

"In the kitchen," Reba called, adding, "Which is kind of part of the living room."

Marti came around the entry wall holding up two bottles of wine. "I didn't know if you wanted red or white, so I brought both," she said.

"Since there are three of us, we may open both," Reba said. "You remember my neighbor Bella."

"The author who doesn't know if she wants to be an author yet," Marti said.

"Did I say that?" Bella asked her.

"No, but I have good instincts about people. You don't seem like one of those people who just has to put their thoughts on paper."

"Umph," Bella replied, as Marti put the bottles on the counter and checked out the culinary creation the girls had just finished.

"Did you guys make this for the three of us?" she asked.

"It was fun," Bella said. "Is it okay if we don't go out to eat?"

"I'm good with this, but it's almost too pretty to pull apart. You need to take a picture before I sample anything."

Reba walked across the room for her phone and did just that.

"Let me get one of you two standing behind it," Marti said. "My next social gathering, you two are making one of these for my guests. Bella, maybe you should go into culinary arts instead of literary arts."

"Marti," Reba said, "Don't be rude."

"I didn't mean to be," she said, "Sorry, Bella."

"Actually, you're not the first person lately to question my path into literary arts as you call it," Bella said.

"Let's open the wine and then take this masterpiece to the coffee table, sit on or near Barney and talk about the career your grandmother chose for you."

Marti snapped a picture of Bella and Reba smiling by the round plate of cheeses, meats, crackers, fruits, nuts and various olives.

"Red or white?" Reba asked as she opened both.

"I'll start with white," Marti said.

"Me, too," Bella added.

As Reba poured the wine, Marti picked up one of the salami rosettes and asked how they made it.

"Maybe I should keep it a secret if by the end of the evening I'm more of a chef than an author."

"Actually," Marti said, with a wrinkled forehead, "I don't get a chef vibe from you either."

"That's good," Bella laughed. "I love cooking as a pastime, but I'd hate spending my days in an industrial kitchen."

"I'm right there with you," Marti said, as she lifted the board and walked across the room. "I got this if you girls bring the wine."

"You're an event planner, right?" Bella said, as they all found a seat near the coffee table. "Doesn't that involve menu decisions and stuff concerning the kitchen."

"Menus, yes," Marti said, "Kitchens, no. I make decisions. Someone else does the work. I took Chip to Las Vegas with me once. He can tell you. When I'm on location, I just boss everyone else around."

"I heard you were busy hustling from place to place, person to person for two days before the event," Reba said.

"Yeah," Marti said, with a nonchalant wave of her hand, "bossing everyone around. No big deal."

Reba gave Bella a look that said, 'don't believe it!'

The girls sampled various foods on the board, commented on the cute wafers Bella found at Fresh Market, and also on the wine Marti said was a gift from a client. After a few minutes, Marti, who was sitting on the floor, pulled a large pillow down, put it behind her back, and leaned back with her glass of wine to eyeball Bella.

"What?" Bella asked.

"I was just wondering who else challenged your literary career path," Marti said.

"It wasn't really a criticism," Bella said. "Will and I were having lunch and he asked me if I really wanted to be a writer and I said no, but I would if it was God's plan for my life."

"You had lunch with Will Carter?" Reba asked at the same time as Marti asked, "Would God expect you to write a book if you're not a writer?"

"Yes," Bella said to Reba, and "I don't know for sure," she said to Marti.

When the room remained quiet, Bella said, "I always thought that God had a specific plan for every life and it was our responsibility to figure out the path he had set for us so we could fulfill our destiny, but after hearing Will's understanding of God and the Bible, I'm not sure what to believe."

"How long have you been dating Will?" Reba asked.

"We're not dating," she answered. "We went to J. Peters one day when I dropped by Carla's office at lunch time and she was busy. Then we've had a couple phone conversations about the Bible. We're not dating."

"You hardly know this guy and you talk on the phone about the Bible?" Reba asked.

"Just a couple times," Bella replied, wondering why she was so uncomfortable with this conversation.

"I find this fascinating," Marti said.

"That she's secretly dating Will Carter?" Reba asked.

"No, that they're not dating and yet they are having deep conversations about God. Don't you think that's interesting?" Marti asked.

"Who called who first?" Reba asked.

"I guess I did," Bella said. "We talked about God at lunch and he was so knowledgeable about the Bible that a few days later I reading and had a question, so I called him."

"He gave you his number?" Reba asked.

"No. I called the office," Bella replied. "He said he wasn't sure of the Bible verse that would make his answer clear, but he'd look it up and call me that night."

"How long did you talk?" Reba asked.

"I don't know," Bella answered. "An hour or so."

"You talked for an hour about the Bible?" Reba demanded.

"Why are you interrogating her?" Marti asked. "So what if they talked about God and the Bible?"

"It's like she's stalking him," Reba said.

"No," Bella said, "The second night we talked, he called me."

"But you're not dating," Reba challenged.

"Reba, lighten up," Marti said, "Are you his mother?"

"Oh my gosh," Bella exclaimed, "Is there something between you and Will? I didn't know."

"No," Reba said, "There's not. I just can't believe you had one lunch date and now you have these deep theological discussions. Who does that if they aren't … you know, dating or engaged or something?"

"Chip and I weren't dating but we spent time together and had long talks," Marti said.

"About God?" Reba asked.

"Neither one of us is really deep when it comes to Bible stuff, but sometimes we talked about things like forgiveness and how God's love is unconditional."

"Forgive me for being surprised," Reba said. "I guess I'm the weird one."

"You're not weird," Marti said, and then added, "Well, being so intense about it was a little weird."

"Sorry," Reba said.

"So, Bella," Marti asked, "what did you mean when you said it is our responsibility to find God's plan for our life?"

"Oh, my God!" Reba exclaimed. "Are we now going to have deep religious conversations?"

"I just thought it was interesting what Bella said," Marti explained, "I think I've always felt a little guilty for missing the plan God had for me."

"Will explained it better than I ever could," Bella said, "So, I won't even try, but it has something to do with not feeling guilty. It's easy to think by our age if your life isn't running smoothly you messed up somewhere along the way."

"Let me just end this conversation by saying that I'm perfectly fine with my life the way it is and I had enough religion in my young years to know it ain't all that great," Reba said, "So, can we now talk about something else?"

"Sure," Marti said, "I met George Strait on Saturday."

"What!" both girls exclaimed together.

"Just was introduced to him and shook his hand," Marti said, smiling because she knew that statement would quickly end the tension in the room. She spent the next twenty minutes answering questions about George.

Chapter 16

Carla was surprised to get a call Tuesday from Olivia.

"Hey," Carla answered, "Are you in town for the storm? Aren't people supposed to leave town, not visit when there is a hurricane threat?"

Olivia laughed. "I'm still in Virginia. I wanted to know if you had heard from Taylor lately."

"I haven't," Carla answered. "Are you worried about her?"

"The last time we talked was the beginning of the summer and she was working on her forensic degree with the hopes of working with you guys. We didn't talk all summer, but I've been trying to get in touch with her for a week and I think her phone is either turned off or disconnected."

"Who else might she be in touch with?" Carla asked.

"I don't know," she replied. "My dad said he hadn't heard from her, so I had DJ ask Rob if they were still connected. Rob said they spoke a few times last spring. She talked about them getting together when her classes ended the end of July, but he never heard from her. He has the same phone number that I have, but he tried to call her anyway. He got the same lack of response, as though her phone is dead."

"Who was she dating?" Carla asked. "You know how gaga she would get over a guy. Maybe she took off with someone and didn't think to let anyone know, or didn't want anyone to know."

"She was usually straight with me," Olivia said. "I'm kind of worried about her."

"She told you what she wanted you to hear," Carla said.

"What?"

"Didn't you ever notice that some of her stories didn't make sense or that one story would contradict another?"

"That's just how Taylor was," Olivia said, "I don't think she lied to me. She was kind of ditsy, so sometimes she got facts confused. That was why I was so surprised she wanted to go into such a detailed job with a serious degree."

"Maybe she was flunking out of forensic classes and was embarrassed, so she isn't telling anyone here what happened."

"I'm not there anymore," Olivia said. "She would tell me and swear me to secrecy. I sometimes had trouble remembering what things she told me were a secret and what things I could talk about."

"I don't know what to tell you," Carla said.

"Can't you just track her phone or something to find out if she's okay?"

Carla laughed. "Yes, but not legally."

"Who's going to snitch on you?" Olivia asked. "I mean, I wouldn't say anything to anyone, but it's like she's just vanished. What if she needs help and can't contact us?"

"You've been reading too many suspense books,' Carla said.

"Like I have time with two little ones to read a book," Olivia said.

"What did DJ say?" Carla asked.

Discouraged, Olivia sighed, "The same thing as you said. He won't ask the guys he knows on base to check on her. I can understand them not bending a rule, but you know her. I'm worried, Carla."

Carla sighed and was silent for a moment. "Do you know the names of any of her family members or a friend from the past we could call?"

"We?" Olivia said. "Does that mean you'll look into it?"

"If you get me something to look into, I'll see what I can do. Do you know her social security number or in what state her driver's license was issued."

"No, but my dad would have that information from her employment resumé. Why didn't I think of that? I'll check with him and get back to you. Thanks, Carla. You're the best!"

Carla hung up and had just turned back to her computer when she got a text from Olivia that read, I just remembered she had a friend at school named Roxie. There can't be that many Roxie's enrolled there. Does that help?

Carla locked her fingers and put her chin on her linked knuckles, as she stared at her computer. She figured she'd be unable to concentrate on her work until she checked the school records. It didn't take her long to find Roxie Rogers from Harpton, Georgia, a small town, northwest of Macon, Georgia, with a population under 9,000. The school wouldn't give her Roxie's phone number, but they would leave her message with Carla's contact information on a message board with the school which would give Roxie the opportunity to call her. She left her name and number and said she was looking for Taylor.

Chapter 17

Marti called Carla the next morning and suggested meeting for dinner at Taproom. They arrived just as Dolley, Mac and Sandy were talking to the hostess. Dolley suggested they get a table for five. Carla agreed before Marti could object.

"It doesn't look like your cousin is working tonight," Sandy said to Marti.

"No," Marti replied, "I watched her kids today so she could work the day shift. Both of them have sore throats."

"That had to be a fun day," Carla said.

"It's enough to keep a girl single," Marti replied.

"Does that mean you're not seeing anyone?" Dolley asked.

"Nothing marriage worthy," Marti replied.

"Evasive answers are smart with this group," Mac smiled.

"I wasn't being evasive, just honest," Marti said, but no one asked her any further questions about her love life.

"However, if we want to gossip," Marti lowered her voice in a conspiratory way, "Did you know that Reba's neighbor, Bella was dating Will?"

"My Will?" Carla asked.

"I'm not sure whose Will he is," Marti said, "but Reba didn't seem too happy about that revelation either."

"I just introduced them a week ago," Carla said.

"She claims they aren't dating, but after your introduction, they had lunch and have been having long phone calls discussing, of all things, God and the Bible. It seems Will is very knowledgeable about it."

"That sounds like a good thing," Sandy said.

"I think it's a little suspicious," Marti told them. "Pretending to be spiritual seems, I don't know, sacrilegious or something."

"Who do you think is pretending?" Dolley asked.

"Did Bella seem like a religious person when you met her? There's something about that girl that bothers me. What about this grandmother who hears from God and bought the condo so her granddaughter, who doesn't write by the way, could move in and become a novelist? No one but me thinks that's odd?"

"Maybe she's just finding her way," Sandy said. "And the idea that Will has studied the Bible makes sense. Tragedies tend to make people turn to God or turn away from God. Losing his wife as he did and then spending time in prison was a traumatic event."

"Something you understand better than most," Carla smiled at her mother.

Chip walked up to the table then and greeted the group. "We're a little light on servers tonight," he said. "Can I take your drink orders?"

The women ordered glasses of wine. Mac ordered a decaf coffee. "Designated driver," he smiled.

Before Chip left the table, he handed Carla a long envelop which she took and put in her purse. "From Tap," he said.

"That was very mysterious," Marti said.

"Just something he wants me to check into," Carla told her.

"Do you do background checks on his employees?" Dolley asked.

"No," she said. "This is a separate matter from the restaurant." When no one spoke, but all eyes were on her, she jokingly said, "And he doesn't suspect Elsa of cheating on him. It's not a family matter."

"That's good to know," Mac said. "I heard they were going to the mountains this week. Chip helped board up their house on the marsh before they left."

"How do you know these things?" his wife asked him.

"I know a lot of things," he said, and winked at the group. "I may be retired, but I still have my sources. That's how I know they have located the man who killed Dasher."

"What?" Sandy said. "They found him? Why didn't Longstreet tell me?"

"I just got the call as we were leaving the house," Mac said. "I asked him if I could tell you and he said yes."

"Why would he not want me to know?" Sandy asked, obviously annoyed.

"I thought he might want to tell you himself, but he said you should know as soon as we knew and that you had just left for Taproom."

"That's why you wanted to come here?" Dolley asked.

"We always eat here," he said, "It was just a coincidence that we were coming at the same time."

"So, tell us what you know." Carla said.

"They knew his name was John Lopez, or at least he had an ID in that name."

"How did they know that?" Marti asked.

"The police located his hotel room by showing his photo and they found an ID and fingerprints," Carla said.

"So, why did it take so long to find him?" Dolley wanted to know.

"John Lopez is a pretty common name and it seemed he might be going by a different name as he had not used his driver's license or any credit cards in that name since the murder. His fingerprints weren't on record, but the hotel clerk described the tattoo on his arm and that led them to a gang symbol in Miami, Florida," Carla said.

"There they found little other than a girlfriend," Mac continued, "who they put a watch on. Monday, she bought a bus ticket to Albuquerque, New Mexico. The LEO's there were waiting for her. They watched her leave the bus station and get into a car with Lopez. They followed them to a quiet neighborhood, and made an uneventful arrest when the couple was walking to the front door of a small house."

"Did he confess to killing Dasher?" Sandy asked.

"He said it was self-defense," Mac said. "He claimed he was only supposed to find the guy staying at the house next door and question him, but when Dasher pulled a gun on him, he panicked and fired to save his own life."

"Do the police believe that story?" Dolley asked.

"No," Mac said, "but he lawyered up, so he is in custody and can't hurt anyone else."

"What about the girlfriend?" Dolley asked.

"They let her go," Mac said. "What she does now is up to her."

"Can you imagine taking a bus across the country to meet the man you are engaged to and have him immediately arrested for murder?" Marti said.

"It wasn't like she hadn't been warned," Carla said.

"But love can be blind," Marti said.

"Or women can be needy," Mac said.

"That's pretty cynical," Dolley said.

"I agree with Mac," Carla said. "She knew he had gang ties, and that the police were looking for him. It's not like he was innocent and turned himself in. He took off across the country and thought he was flying under the radar. If that were me, I would have cut him loose and hocked the ring."

"What if that had been Mike?" Marti asked.

"Mike hunts bad guys. He doesn't hang out with them," she stated.

"Are you okay?" Dolley asked Sandy, putting her hand over hers.

"I'm just taking it all in," she said. "I guess I don't need body guards anymore."

"I guess you don't," Dolley smiled.

Carla exchanged a look with Mac that said whoever was looking for Rob or Longstreet was probably still looking, but neither said anything.

By Friday night, as the winds picked up along the coast of South Carolina, the police had extradited John Lopez back to Myrtle Beach and convinced him that the only way he had a chance of anyone believing his story was if he gave them the name of the guy who ordered him to "find" the guy next door. John claimed all he knew was the man was in his fifties, very handsome, and people knew him only as Dr. Martin. John said he wasn't from Florida or South Carolina. He heard he lived somewhere out west, but he didn't know where or anything else about him. He only met the guy the one time. When asked if anyone in the Baby Demons had contact with this Dr. Martin, John claimed to not know who the Baby Demons were. That was an obvious lie.

Carla was glad they had the guy who killed Dasher, but they still had very little information that would make her mother completely safe. She also knew her crew and Longstreet were not letting this go. She knew Longstreet was torn between staying close to protect Sandy and leaving town to draw whoever was looking for him or Rob to a different location. He decided in case someone was still watching the houses, he'd have Rob come visit and then together they'd fly to Virginia, but they'd wait until the storm had moved out to sea and/or past the DC/Virginia area.

Late Friday night, Mike walked into Carla's office. "We should go," he said. "The wind and rain is getting worse."

"The forecast has lowered the threat from a hurricane to a tropical storm," she said, "but I'm almost at a place I can stop. Just one more click." She dramatically hit the send key and waited.

"Shoot," she said, "we might as well go. I'll try a different tactic tomorrow."

"What are you working on?" he asked as she locked the front door.

"Finding the elusive Dr. Martin," she answered before they both ran for Mike's car.

Chapter 18

Dr. Martin Ashbury lived in a remote area above Denver, Colorado. His large, state-of-the-art log home did not reflect his public persona as a quiet, studious college professor. Most of the exclusive group who were invited to the lavish parties he threw, knew him only as Doc. Many of them assumed him to be a medical doctor, but really didn't care. What they loved was the fact that they were part of his inner circle, and understood the need for discretion. The secrecy was attributed to his unassuming personality. The few who knew he was a college professor believed his great wealth had been inherited. What the inner circle knew for sure was that he threw great parties with gourmet food, expensive booze, cigars and wine, and quality marijuana and drugs for those who wanted the enhanced experience of flying high, as Doc would say. Doc never made use of the weed and pills he provided. In fact, his drink of choice was a high-end bourbon, of which he only imbibed when he was smoking one of his valued Nicaraguan cigars.

Tonight's party was in full swing and dinner would be announced any minute. He checked his watch and looked to the grand staircase that descended from the second-floor balcony. Diana knew he was a stickler for punctuality. Making him wait was one of her few flaws, which he usually contributed to her youth, although tonight he wondered if it wasn't some power-play on her part. They had argued this morning about the need for her to stay on his property unless he escorted her to a place of his choosing, usually on his private plane which was housed in his private hanger near his private airstrip.

Diana had been with him for several months and was getting tired of the isolation. He'd have to find a remedy for that because he believed he might actually be in love this time. In fact, it was often her spunk and determination that excited him. There had been times he had angered her in order to enjoy her independence and his ability to tame her with romantic words and gestures until she was again beautiful, soft putty in his capable hands.

Martin was ready to go after her as the dinner bell rang and Diana appeared at the top of the stairs, a vision of angelic beauty. Momentary, he forgot his guests and wanted nothing more than to climb up that staircase and take what was his. He was sure he had never loved like this before. She smiled and made eye-contact with him as she seemingly floated down the stairs. For a second, he forgot the crowd watching them, who had stopped on their way to the dining hall to look up. When he realized they were watching his reaction to her as much as they were watching Diana, he was embarrassed. He did not wish to be considered a fool in love, but there was nothing to do now but shrug his shoulders and gin, making his guests nod, as they turned with smiling faces and entered the room with the grand tables and ornate chandeliers.

As she reached the bottom steps and he walked toward her, he was torn between chastising her for being late again and complimenting her on her impeccable style and beauty. Because he wanted the night to end well for him, he chose the latter.

"You look ravishing, my love," he said, as he bent to kiss her cheek. "I'm not sure I like every man in the room wishing he were in my shoes."

"No worries," she purred, "I only have eyes for you. I was only late because I wanted to please you."

"Maybe we can end this party early for the same reason," he said, taking her hand and tucking it into his bent elbow. "May I escort the most gorgeous woman here into the dining hall?"

"It is my pleasure, Martin" she responded, dropping her eyes, and then coyly glancing sideways at him. "Tonight, as always, I am all yours."

He loved it when she spoke to him that way, as though they were a couple in one of the Elizabethan literature classes he taught. He cleared his throat, to bring himself back into control. He would not look smitten again in front of his guests.

After dinner, there was a quartet playing in the ballroom for dancing, along with private rooms on the first floor for whatever purpose his guests might desire. Two of the men had responded to his invitation that they would be available, but that they were not dating anyone at the moment. For those men, Martin had, as expected, provided dates that arrived together in a stretch limousine. The girls were young, shapely, and experienced. He generously paid for their service, and was never disappointed. In fact, before Diana, he had used the same service himself, and had been impressed with each girl's grace and conversational skills.

Around 11:30, Martin whispered to Diana that he had to go down to the wine cellar. He said it might take up to an hour, so she was to enjoy herself as his hostess.

"I can assure you everything offered is quality, but be careful, and no cigars," he teased. "I don't want you to smell like one of the guys when we make love."

"Oh, Marty," she giggled. "You know I'm not interested in any of your stuff. I'll just have another glass of wine."

Marty discreetly patted her bottom as he turned to leave her for a while. Diana decided to use the ladies room before getting her fourth glass of wine. The room off the foyer had a double sink, an Oscar de la Renta bench, and three enclosed stalls. Diana used one of the stalls, and came out to wash her hands and refresh her lipstick.

"Doc sure throws the best parties," the girl who was washing her hands said to Diana.

"Yes, he does," she agreed. "He loves entertaining guests."

"I was one of his special guests one time," the girl smiled. "When I got here, I was disappointed he had already acquired you."

"Acquired me?" Diana asked, with a raised eyebrow.

"Oh. I'm sorry," she quickly amended, "I thought you were just a date. I didn't realize you were more to him. I didn't mean any offense."

The girl quickly dried her hands and hurried from the room, wondering if she had ruined her opportunity to ever be invited her again.

Diana sat down on the padded bench. She wondered what her future held. Would she one day be one of those girls? Not an escort, of course, but one more girl that Marty had tired of. Their relationship felt like more to her. She knew she had never loved anyone like she loved Marty. It was so much more than the expensive clothes and trips and exciting sex. He had taught her culture and introduced her to things she had only dreamed about. Of course, his age made him more experienced than her in so many ways, but there was something more. She read it in his eyes when he looked at her; like tonight as she came down the stairs. It wasn't just his handsome face or smooth moves and words when they were in bed. It was little things that made her feel loved. She hated knowing the girl in the emerald green dress had also been with him, but she chose to believe his time with that girl had only been about sex. After all, she wasn't a child. He was more than twenty years her senior. Of course, he had been with lots of women, but she and Marty had so much more. She and Marty were really in love; the kind of love that sometimes just cuddled, the kind that lasted a lifetime.

In the wine cellar, Marty was in deep conversation with one of his guests who said, "John Lopez was captured in Albuquerque and extradited to Myrtle Beach. How much can he hurt you?"

"He can't," Marty told him. "I didn't even tell him my name. He knows nothing about me, where I'm from, who I'm connected to. That's why I chose an amateur nobody."

"Obviously! A professional wouldn't have shot the wrong guy and he wouldn't have sent his girlfriend money to come to him."

"Oh, man," Marty said, "What a fool. But he can talk all he wants. He doesn't know me and all he knows about his target was the address of where he lived. I didn't even tell him the guy's name."

"Then how was he supposed to get it right if he didn't even know who he was after? Even a smart nobody would have wanted to know who he was supposed to kill. I think Diana has clouded your judgement. You used to be better than this."

"She has nothing to do with that side of me."

"I saw how you looked at her tonight," the guest said. "A man in love can be a fool. Either wise up or get an ugly girlfriend. She may be a great lay, but is she worth dying or going to prison for?"

Diana was watching the door to the lower level when a man she recognized but had never been introduced to came out, looked around without seeing her, and left by the front door. When Marty came through the door a few minutes later, she could tell he was upset. She waited until he was in the crowd looking for her to appear at his side.

"Where have you been?" he asked with a smile.

Diana held up her glass of wine and said, "Just mingling. "Did you know Michael and Babs are going to have a baby?"

"No," he said, "Are they happy about it?"

"They are very excited," Diana said, and then asked, "Is Babs her real name?"

"It's the only thing I've ever heard her called," he replied. "What time is it?"

"A little after midnight," she said, "Why?"

"I'm ready for this party to be over," he said.

"Is everything alright?" she asked.

"No. I'm ready to go upstairs with my girl and there are a bunch of people hanging around eating my food and drinking my booze." He pulled her close and said in a conspiratorial way, "Make them go away."

Diana laughed. "We could send the band home," she suggested.

"Great idea," he said, letting go of her and walking toward the music room.

She watched him say something to the band leader who nodded. Then he disappeared toward the kitchen. When he reappeared, he took her hand and as they wandered through the main living area, he congenially spoke to most of the guests, hoping they were having a good time. Then they sauntered with her hand inside his arm, covered with his other hand. It seemed they were headed to the back patio, but Marty made a quick turn and pulled her up the back stairway until they were at the top and quietly running down the hall to their suite.

"What are we doing?" Diana asked in a whisper, as Marty shut their door and locked it.

"We left the party to have one of our own," he smiled.

"But it's your party," she said. "Can you do that?"

"It's our party," he corrected, "and we can do whatever we want."

"But what about the guests?"

"I told the band to stop in 45 minutes, and Albert to make sure everyone left by lowering the lights after the music stopped. If anyone asks about us, he is to say I got a call about a death in the family."

Diana laughed as he grabbed her by the waist, pulled her close and nuzzled her neck.

"That's terrible," she told him.

"You don't like this?" he asked, enjoying her giggle.

"I love it, but can you really leave your own party?"

"You think they won't come back?" he asked, stopping to look at her face.

"Maybe I don't care," she said, with a twinkle in her eye.

"That's my girl," Marty said, picking her up and dropping her on the bed.

"My dress," she said.

"What about it?" he asked.

"It's expensive. You're going to ruin it."

"Then let's get you out of it," he smiled.

It was 5:00am when Diana woke in an empty bed. When she looked around the room, she saw Marty sitting in the dark, looking out at a dark sky. She quietly got out of bed and walked to where he sat. Instinctively, she stood behind him and began massaging his temples. He gave a soft moan.

"Does it help?" she asked softly.

"Help what?" he sighed.

"It doesn't change whatever is bothering you, but I thought it might help the headache," she said.

"It does," he whispered.

Diana didn't say anything, but continued the circular motion with her fingers.

"I love you," Marty said.

"You have never said that to me before," she replied, her fingers never stopping their gentle motion.

"I know," he said. "I've never said that to anyone."

Her fingers stopped. "I don't believe you," she said.

Marty took her hand and brought her around to sit on his lap. "It's true," he told her. "I'm not a good person, Diana. I've lived my life for myself, doing and taking what I wanted, but it's different now. I'm different now, and it's all because of you."

Diana put her hands on both sides of Marty's face. "I love you," she said. "I love this handsome face, and" she said, moving her one hand to his chest, "I love this heart."

"It's not what you think," he said. "I'm not what you think."

"Oh, but you are," she told him. "I don't know what you do besides teach students and I don't really care. What I do know is that you love me. You accept me to be what you see, and I accept you to be what I see. That's all that matters to me. Marty! You cuddle with me."

Marty laughed. "That's easy. There's something cuddleable about you."

"Is that a word?"

"If it isn't, it should be," he said.

"Do you want to tell me what happened in the wine cellar?" I'm a good listener?"

"What do you mean?"

"I saw that man come up before you and leave. You were upset and you needed to be with me, just me. You cannot know how much that means to me. I don't need to know, but I'm a good listener if you want to talk."

Taking her face in his hands, he looked into her eyes. "What I want is for you to forget that guy and let me all your eyes need to see. Let me fill your life with anything and everything your heart desires. I can do that. I promise I can."

"You already do fill my life," she said, "but there is something I'd like to do."

"Anything, as long as it's with me," he winked.

"I want to see the ocean."

"Okay," he said. "How does the Mediterranean sound?"

"It sounds delightful."

"Then, we'll leave tomorrow," he said.

"You mean like in a few hours?" she asked.

"No. I have some calls to make. Can you be ready in 24 hours?"

"I don't have a bathing suit here," she said.

"We'll buy one there, unless you want to stop in Paris to shop on the way."

"I love you," she squealed, throwing her arms around his neck. "I promise to massage your temples any time you want."

Marty laughed.

"And I promise to cuddle any time you want." Suddenly solemn, Diana said, "Do you think we can keep those promises? At moments like this, it seems so easy."

"I think we can try," he said, seriously. "I want to give you a lifetime of moments like this, Diana. If I ever fail you, know it wasn't my intent."

"Me, too, you," she said, and gently kissed him.

"I'm not sad anymore," Marty said, lifting her and carrying her back to bed. "Let's get some sleep. We have a busy day tomorrow."

Gently putting her in the middle of the bed, Marty lay behind her and wrapped an arm around her waist, drawing her back against his chest. He knew he was not a good guy, but at moments like these, he wished he was.

Chapter 19

The storm along the South Carolina coast produced heavy winds and rain, but the eye of the storm stayed just off shore and it moved quickly up the coast. Waccamaw Drive in front of Sandy's, Longstreet's, and Dolley's homes was flooded for a while, but the water receded by mid-afternoon, leaving everything coated with a layer of wet sand. The locals knew they would be back to normal by Monday.

Sandy and Longstreet took the dogs for a walk on the beach as they heard the trucks clearing sand from the street.

"Oh look," Sandy said, as she pointed out over the water. "It seems God always provides a rainbow after one of our storms."

"Once again," Longstreet said, "It wasn't as drastic as the weather stations forecasted."

"I think they have to prepare everyone for the worst, just in case," Sandy told him. "It gives people less to complain about."

Longstreet laughed, "It's good to see your positive outlook returning. I was worried about you."

"Really?" she asked. "Well, it feels good to have the bad guy behind bars. I hope he has to stay there."

"He will," Longstreet said.

"And you can go back to sleeping in your own bed instead of my sofa," she smiled.

"Your sofa is actually comfortable," he said, "but if you don't mind, I'd like to leave Ike at your place at night for a while."

"Why?" she asked, stopping and turning a troubled expression toward him. "I thought I was out of danger now."

"You know me," he tried to downplay his concerns, "I just want to be able to sleep in my own bed and for a while it will be easier if Ike is with you."

Sandy wasn't sure she believed him. "You'd tell me if there was still a threat to my life, wouldn't you?"

"Yes," he said. "I don't believe anyone is looking to do you harm. I'm not sure Lopez was out to get you in the first place. I think he had been given a job to find Rob or me and he blew it."

"What would have happened if he had found you at your house?" she asked.

Longstreet laughed. "That's assuming he got past Ike."

"If you leave him with me," she said, "you know I can't walk the two of them."

"I'll still be in charge of Ike," he said. "He'll still be with me during the day. I'll just put him on your porch with Hero at night. I think Hero might suffer some withdraw symptoms if I change his sleeping habits too abruptly."

Sandy laughed. "You might be right. When you finally go back to the mountains with Ike, I may end up with Hero in my bed. Thanks a lot."

"For stormy nights or nightmares, he might be a good cuddler," Longstreet said.

"I'm not afraid of storms," Sandy told him. "And I'm hoping the nightmares are gone with John Lopez being in prison."

"Have you still been having them?" Longstreet asked

"Not as often and not as bad as before," she said. "I haven't had one since they caught Lopez."

"Good," was all he said. "Want to go out for lunch today? Make sure the rest of the South Strand fared as well as we did?"

After days of preparing for and worrying about the storm, and then the two nights and a day of weathering the storm, it appeared everyone was out experiencing the sunny skies and dry warm air. Since Taproom closed on Mondays, Sandy and Longstreet drove to the Marsh Walk.

"Dead Dog Saloon?" Longstreet asked, as they passed The Beaver Bar.

"How about Neal's Creekhouse?" she suggested.

"Haven't been there but once," Longstreet said. "Let's do it."

The parking lot wasn't too crowded yet, so they were able to get a table outside. The water, as expected, was high.

"The other time I was here was low tide," Longstreet said. "It was only mud there."

"Even without the storm, tide makes a big difference," she said, as they each perused the menus. "What are you going to order?"

"I think I'll try the Flounder basket," he said. "If I'm heading back to the mountains one of these days, I need to get my fix of good seafood."

"Are you planning on going soon?" she asked.

"I talked to Rob this weekend," he began.

"Rambo?" she asked.

"Yeah," He's coming here this week and then we are going to fly up to Virginia together."

"Does he still keep in touch with Taylor?" she asked.

"I don't think so," Longstreet said. "Do you think I should try something else?"

"Are you seriously asking me or changing the subject?"

"I'm seriously asking," he said.

"Everything I've ever ordered here was good, so go for whatever looks good to you today."

He read over the menu until their server arrived. Sandy ordered the Rueben sandwich with Tater Tots. Longstreet decided on the Shrimp and Flounder Combo.

"Carla seems to be awfully busy these days," Sandy said. "When I talk to her, I sometimes feel like her mind is somewhere else. Do you know what they are working on now that John Lopez has been found?"

"I think they have a lot of projects going, both private ones and police business."

"Taylor originally said she was going to get a forensic degree and join them. I wonder if Carla has heard from her. If they are that busy, they could probably use some help."

"Carla hasn't said anything to me," Longstreet responded. "Have you heard anything about Barb and Jake? I don't think Tap's too happy that Jake is back."

"I think everyone is a little skeptical of Jake."

"What's the problem?"

"Jake was on drugs when Tap first met him. He seemed sincere about wanting a second chance and Tap gave him one.

Jake's a fun guy. He did well behind the bar and the customer's loved him."

"What changed?"

"He and Barb got married. He became an instant dad. They bought a house and Barb gets pregnant. Suddenly, he has a greater financial responsibility, and a family counting on him. Barb couldn't work as many hours at Taproom, so it was up to Jake to make more money. I think maybe he became overwhelmed or he felt trapped. I don't know, but the next thing you know, Barb seems unhappy and stressed. Maybe that was her reaction to the same things Jake was reacting to, or maybe it was a reaction to the changes in Jake. I'm not sure."

"But he came back," Longstreet said.

"Jake had an affair and rumor has it the woman dumped him and somehow got him fired."

"They worked together?"

"Yeah. I think Tap worries Jake is just back because in the moment he had nowhere else to go. He's afraid, when the pressure gets to Jake, he'll be gone again, leaving a devastated Barb and brokenhearted, confused children."

"It's not easy to be everything to everyone," Longstreet said. "I failed as a husband and father. It's a terrible feeling. You watch the rest of the world make it work and you are filled with anger, guilt and regret, besides the people you've disappointed. I hope he figures it out. I've seen guys in his situation go from marriage to marriage leaving a trail of broken people in the wake."

"Hey, what are you two kids up to?" Mike asked, as he and Carla walked up to their table.

"Want to join us?" Sandy asked.

"Yes!" Carla said, before Mike could respond. "Mike was leading us to those surfboard tables with backless stools."

"That's where we sat last time and had a good time," he said.

"I'd rather have a good time in a chair with a back," Carla said. "Besides, we haven't seen these guys out for a while. It was good we didn't get the hurricane they were forecasting at first. We drove down Waccamaw this morning. It looks like they mostly have sand to plow."

"Yeah," Sandy said. "We didn't see any flooding either."

The four had a nice visit together. For part of the lunch, Sandy and Carla talked about family as Mike and Longstreet talked about an old mutual friend Mike had recently heard from.

"Have either of you heard from Taylor lately?" Sandy asked. "Didn't she talk about working for you once she finished her degree?"

"She did, but I haven't heard from her yet," Carla said. When her phone rang, she looked at the number. "I think I'd better take this call," she said and walked around to the parking lot where it was quiet and she could hear. "Hello?" she answered.

"Is this Carla Campbell?" a young voice asked.

"Yes," she answered, "Is this Roxanne Winters?"

"It is," she replied. "You left a message that you were looking for Taylor. Has something happened to her?"

"I was afraid you weren't going to call," Carla said.

"I don't check that message board all that often," Roxie apologized.

"That's fine," Carla said, "A few of us have been trying to call Taylor, but her phone seems to be disconnected or something. We couldn't get through and thought you might know if she broke her phone or met a guy or something."

"Are you the Carla she was thinking about working for?" Roxie asked.

"Yes," Carla said. "I should have stayed more in touch, but we have been busy with work. Was she enjoying her classes?"

"I don't think so," Roxie said. "As she got farther into the program, she seemed more and more discouraged, so I wasn't that surprised when she met this guy and told me she was going to drop out of school to move in with him."

"Why would moving in with him result in dropping out of school?"

"I asked her the same thing," Roxie said, "and she got angry with me. That was the last time we talked. I tried to call her, but she wouldn't take my calls or call me back. I even texted her a couple times, but after a week or so, the text didn't go through. I guess she's with that guy, unless you know something I don't'.

"I was hoping you'd have more information," Carla told her. "Her friend Olivia has been trying to get hold of her, too. It seems she has ghosted everyone."

"Do you think she's okay?" Roxie asked.

"It's Taylor," Carla tried to sound positive. "She's probably with that guy and will just show up one of these days. If you hear from her, will you let me know?"

"Of course," Roxie said, "And the same here. I'll worry about her now until I hear she's okay."

"She probably is," Carla said, "but as soon as I know anything ... can I reach you on this number?"

"Yes, it's my cell," Roxie said. "Taylor didn't seem happy before she dissed everyone. I'm going to trust that she's found a guy who makes her happy."

"Did she say anything about him?" Carla asked. "Like his first or last name, what he looks like, where he's from? Was it a guy from school?"

"I don't think he was from our school," Roxie said. "All she said was he was cute, sexy and he understood."

"Understood what?" Carla asked.

"I thought she meant he understood her dropping out of school. Do you think he's some loser that did something to her?"

"Taylor was always smart and a hard worker," Carla said. "I don't see her moving in with a bum. Can you think of anything we could trace?"

"Like what?"

"A phone bill, or a doctor she saw, or something like that?"

"No," Roxie told her, "And my classes are almost over. I graduate this quarter, so I'm going home to Harpton."

"Harpton, Georgia?"

"Yes," Roxie said, "It's such a small town, I'm surprised you've heard of it."

"I haven't," Carla told her, "It was just a guess. Thanks for calling me back, Roxie. I'll let you know when we hear from her or if I find out anything."

"Thank you, Ms. Campbell. I'll ask around at school, too."

"Maybe one of us will get lucky so we can stop worrying," Carla told her.

By the time she hung up, Mike was by her side.

"Nothing?' he asked

"Nothing," she answered.

"Let's go back to work," he said, draping an arm around her shoulder.

Carla decided when she got back in the office to treat Taylor like a missing person. Thanks to Tap, she had her social security number. She had already tried the number and address that Taylor had listed as belonging to her parents, but it was phony. When Carla looked the address up on Google Maps, it showed a strip mall. The fact that she had lied might be a good sign. If she was less responsible than they had all thought, she probably went off the grid willingly.

Chapter 20

Tuesday, Wednesday and Thursday were cloudy and rainy. Longstreet had been sleeping back at his own house, but every night he dropped off Ike on the porch to sleep by Hero. Some nights, he would come in and visit for a while. Some nights, he'd merely knock on the door to say Ike was on the porch and he'd see her the next day.

Friday morning, Longstreet put Ike on his own back porch and left for the airport to pick up Rob. Since it was sunny and nice, Sandy decided to walk Hero to the coffee shop on Atlantic Avenue. Aaron still owned the place, so they chatted a little between customers. As she and Hero left, she thought about how long she had been at the beach. When she first started walking to the Coffee Grounds, she had Jasper on a leash, and Carla was missing. That seemed so long ago now. Her runaway daughter was now a mature, wise, business owner with a good marriage. As she walked, she thanked God for the work he had done in their lives.

Sandy approached the intersection daydreaming about the past, when suddenly she was aware of a disturbance. It sounded like a shot was fired, and the next thing she knew a car slammed into the person in front of her. As Sandy went backwards, she thought of Patsy.

A few minutes later, Longstreet approached the ocean on Atlantic Blvd. As Rob was telling him about a new gun he had purchased, their attention was drawn to the commotion at the intersection by the Garden City pier. Longstreet's heart raced as he saw the center of attention was a bloody body being protected by Hero. Longstreet slammed on his brakes as both men were out of the car, sprinting toward the small group of people around the body.

"Hero," he commanded, "at ease!"

The anxious dog looked his way, but didn't respond to his command. He was not letting anyone near the body on the ground. As Longstreet heard an approaching siren, he realized there were two bodies on the ground; both were covered in blood and not moving. The one on the bottom was Sandy.

"It's okay, Hero," Longstreet said in a quiet voice. "I'm here. You can be at ease." He immediately put his finger on Sandy's neck and found a pulse. The man on top of her had none.

Looking at the faces watching him and the dog, he demanded, "What happened?"

"Are you guys cops?" one man asked.

"Close enough," Rob replied. "Did anyone see what happened?"

An older man took a step forward, but stopped when Hero growled.

Longstreet linked his thumb into Hero's collar and massaged the dog's neck with his fingers, nodding for the man to continue.

"It was a hit and run," he said. "My wife and I were paying our tab at Sam's Corner when we heard the gunshots."

"Gunshots?" Longstreet asked. "They were shot?"

"We didn't see anything," his wife said, "When we ran out, they were on the ground, but the dog wouldn't let us near them."

"I saw the car," the younger man said. "It was white with a black stripe down the side."

"And it didn't stop?" Longstreet questioned.

"I saw it too," another man said. "It was parked by the pier and when the man started to cross the street, it pulled out fast, just hit the guy and kept going."

"I thought there were gun shots," Longstreet said.

The man shrugged and indicated the headphones now around his neck. "I wasn't paying any attention, but I had noticed the license plate when it was parked."

"You got the plate number?" Longstreet said, as two police cars and an ambulance screeched to the scene.

"They were South Carolina plates that read 2BOOBS. That's why I remembered them."

The EMT's ran to the bodies. One officer took a few quick photos, and then the body on top of Sandy was carefully turned over. To Longstreet's relief, it was immediately evident that there had been shots but they had only hit the man who was dead. Sandy's clothes were bloody and she was unconscious, but no apparent gunshot wounds. The EMT's were immediately at her side.

The police moved the crowd back from the bodies, as Sandy was transferred to the ambulance and the other body was covered, waiting for the second rig to arrive.

Hero did not like them lifting Sandy, and Longstreet struggled to control him.

"I'm her friend and this is her dog," he told the officer who seemed to be in charge. "Where will they be taking her?"

"Waccamaw Hospital," the one EMT said.

"What happened?" the lead officer asked him.

"I drove up after it happened," Longstreet said, indicating his car obstructing traffic at the light.

"Then I need you to move your car and let me talk to someone who saw what happened," he said. "And get that dog away from here or I'll impound him. He's been traumatized and is ready to attack anyone who moves."

Longstreet had enough information and his first concern was Sandy's condition. He would deal with what happened later. Hero was not about to get into Longstreet's car, so Rob drove the short distance to Sandy's home. Longstreet ran back with Hero and called Dolley as he ran. She said she and Mac would call Carla and meet him at the hospital.

Longstreet knew that until Carla got there, no one would be given much information from the front desk in Emergency, so he waited for the EMT's to exit the back entrance.

"Is she stable?" Longstreet asked. "I'm her fiancé," he lied.

"She's not conscious, but she was not bleeding externally," the younger one said, looking at Longstreet. "It appears she was knocked backwards. She has contusions on her one arm and shoulder. Her head hit the ground. They'll do x-rays and scans to determine if there is any internal damage."

The older EMT came out the hospital door and shouted, "You shouldn't be talking to him. That's not your job. Get in the rig!"

The young guy seemed unphased, and said, "She'll probably be okay, Mister. I have a fiancé, also."

It was six hours before Sandy was moved to a room. She was awake, but groggy. After the MRI showed no brain damage, they had given her pain medication.

Rob drove to Mike's office to see what he could find out from the police, but Longstreet stayed at the hospital with Carla, Dolley and Mac. When Sandy was settled in her room, Carla was admitted first with the officer who had told Longstreet to get lost.

Longstreet, Dolley and Mac stood at the door to the room. It was evident that Sandy was hurting and struggling to answer the officer's questions.

"I took Hero for coffee," she said. "We were walking home when there were gunshots and the man standing before me at the curb was hit. He started to fall forward, but the car hit him, making him spin around and fall into me. He knocked me to the sidewalk. I heard Hero bark and then I heard nothing. I woke up in the emergency room."

"Did you see the driver of the car?"

Sandy squinted as though trying to remember. "No," she said. "It all happened so fast. I wasn't paying attention to that car. I don't even know where it came from. The light changed and there seemed to be no traffic on Waccamaw as the man in front of us started to cross the street."

"Us?" the officer asked.

"Hero and I," she said, turning to Carla. "Is he okay?"

"He's fine," Carla said. "We'll let him stay at Longstreet's with Ike tonight."

"I'd like to go home tonight," she said.

"Your head hit the ground pretty hard," Carla told her. "They want to keep you here overnight for observation."

Sandy closed her eyes and sighed.

"I think she's told you all she knows," Carla told the police officer. "If she remembers anything new, we'll let you know. Did they find the car or the driver?"

"Not yet," he said, handing Carla his card, as he turned to leave.

"Detective Baker," the officer said, not looking happy to see Laurie standing in the doorway with the others. "Checking up on me?"

"No," Laurie said, "Sandy's a friend. I was checking up on her."

"She seems to have a lot of those," he sneered, as he walked into the hallway to leave.

"Yes, she does," Laurie smiled to the group as they entered her room. "How the patient?" he asked.

No one believed he was there for mere personal reasons.

"Do you know anything yet?" Mac asked him.

"It seems the striping on the car was peel and stick vinyl that was quickly removed and the vanity plate was stolen off an old, black, Chrysler Valiant. No one is sure what make the hit and run car was, only that it too was an older model sedan."

"Was the victim the target?"

"It seems so," Laurie said. "We don't know much about him yet; no record or past violations, but he did have Longstreet's card in his pocket."

"My card?" Longstreet stepped forward. "What's his name?"

"Justin Shoemaker," Laurie answered. "Know him?"

"Never heard that name," Longstreet said, "What else do you know about him?"

"Not much, yet."

"Can you send us what you have?" Carla asked. "We'll put Andrew on it."

"The other reason I'm here," he smiled. "I already shot Andrew an email. I figured you'd want to be in the loop on this one."

"You know we do," Mac said. "What else can we do?"

"I don't like that she's been witness to two crimes in the last couple months," Laurie said, looking to confirm that Sandy was asleep. "I hate coincidences, but if the shooter was targeting Sandy, it's an amateurish hit. We don't know if the victim had Longstreet's card because he wanted to consult with him or if Longstreet was his target."

"Was the victim carrying?" Mac asked.

"No," Laurie said, "and he wasn't licensed to carry, nor did he own any legal guns. Of course, many guns are not registered, so he may have owned one or more."

"Where does he live?" Carla asked.

"His driver's license is from Colorado," Laurie said.

"Colorado?" Mac asked.

"I thought the same thing," Laurie said. "I asked Andrew to check for any possible Vegas or Barclay connections."

"That could lead to either Longstreet or my mother," Carla said.

"Make sure she's not alone," Laurie said, as he walked toward the door. "We've put her address on a watch list. There will be extra cars cruising Garden City. The problem is, most of the cars in that area have out-of-state license plates, so keep a heads up for anything suspicious."

"You know we will," Mac said.

Since Sandy was asleep, everyone but Carla left. The small group of three came upon Mike and Rob as they walked toward the hospital. In the warm summer air, they talked about strategy. Mike had been at the office when Andrew got the info from Detective Baker. He suspected his analyst would work all night. Everyone was taking this very personally. They didn't like family being in danger. After a short parking lot conversation, they said good-night and went their separate ways. There didn't seem to be much more they could do tonight.

The following morning, Sandy was released from the hospital. Carla had agreed to bring her to Dolley's home first. Shortly after Dolley had Sandy situated on the balcony with a glass of sweet tea and a bakery muffin, Carla left. A short time later, Julie and Chris arrived.

"Oh my," Sandy said. "You two shouldn't have spent all that money to fly here. Look at me. I'm fine."

Julie walked over, hugged her mother and looked into her eyes. "You do not look fine," she said. "Anyway, would you want us to look like we didn't care? Mitch's plane lands in an hour. We told him we'd pick him up."

"How did you find out so soon?" Sandy asked.

"Carla called us last night, of course," Julie said, as Chris walked up and took Sandy's hand.

"Who's Carla?" Sandy asked.

When everyone looked appalled, she laughed, and said, "Got ya!"

"Don't do that to us!" Julie scolded. "I about had a heart attack."

Mac walked in from the den and shook hands with Chris before giving Julie a hug.

"Where is Carla?" Julie asked. "She didn't answer her cell."

"I sent her home to sleep," Sandy said. "She sat in a hospital chair by my bed the entire night."

"It was a recliner and I slept almost as much as you did," Carla called from the doorway as she entered Dolley home.

"You didn't answer my call," Julie said, hugging her older sister.

"I was probably in the shower," Carla said, her hair still slightly damp. "When does Mitch get in?"

"I was thinking," Mac said. "Chris and I can go get Mitch and let you ladies visit."

"That's a wonderful idea Mac," Dolley said. "Maybe I'll have you pick up lunch on your way home."

"Just call me and let me know when and where," he told her. "I think Chris and I will go ahead and leave."

"It's kind of early to go now," Carla said.

"We'll be fine," Mac said, as Chris kissed Julie's cheek and followed Mac out the door. Once they were by Mac's car, he added, "I thought we'd stop and pick up Longstreet on our way."

Chris had only met these guys a few times, but he had been in DJ's class at Quantico, so between DJ and his brother-in-law Mike, he had heard stories of them all. It was a bit intimidating, but he's was thrilled to be included. He said very little on the trip to the airport as Mac and Longstreet compared notes and discussed scenarios. Some of their strategies did not seem to include the police. Longstreet took a couple calls from Mike or

Rob who were at the office where Andrew and Ben were busy analyzing information and looking for leads.

Chapter 21

Mitch, Julie and Chris stuck around for the weekend. It was like a little family reunion that Sandy enjoyed, but the pain pills made her sleepy. However, without them, she couldn't follow conversations well. She knew her children were concerned, but she was doing the best she could. Dolley insisted on keeping her at her house, so Longstreet kept a restless Hero with him and Rob. Julie and Chris slept at Sandy's, and Mitch had Dolley's smaller guest room.

By Monday, Sandy's bruises were dark purple. Since the kids were gone, and everyone else back to work on the case, Dolley insisted she sleep as much as possible. Sandy protested, but it didn't take much encouragement for her to fall back asleep. Carla, Mike and Longstreet all promised to come for dinner. Of course, Rob and Hero were included.

Late that afternoon, Andrew walked into Carla's office as she stood up from her chair, swore, and banged her fist upon her desk.

"I'm guessing that was a dead end," Andrew said.

"I am so frustrated. Everything seems to lead to a dead end," she said. "We never get any closer to a motive in any of these cases; not Dasher's death, not the hit and run shooting, not even Adam Chesterton's father's case. Plus, who commits a hit and run after shooting their victim?"

"That's the most puzzling to me also," he said. "I don't think we even know the basics of that case yet."

"What do you mean?"

As Carla sat back at her desk, Andrew took a seat, leaning back as though he were about to have a leisurely smoked cigar.

"Well, the reality is we don't know who killed Justin Shoemaker or if he was the intended target."

"You think it was my mother?" Carla asked, not knowing if she wanted to hear his answer.

"I just said I don't know, but let's think about what happened," he said.

"What happened when?" Mike asked, as he sauntered into his wife's office.

"Andrew thinks Mom might have been the target of the hit and run," Carla said, as Mike took a seat.

"No," Andrew said, "I said we need to brainstorm some ideas. Why does someone take the time and the risk to commit a hit and run when you have already put three rounds in a guy's chest? That's the first fact I haven't been able to get past."

"Maybe to make sure he's dead," Carla surmised.

"Three to the chest? If he isn't dead at the scene, he will be shortly. The coroner believed the first shot to the heart killed the guy. What does that tell you? Sandy said he had already started to cross the street."

"That he was a good shot," Mike offered.

"A bulls eye to the heart on a moving target from an odd angle? I think our shooter was a pro. He would have been confident that he got the guy, so why run him down?" Andrew waited for a reply.

"He wasn't the target," Mike stated.

"That's ridiculous," Carla stated. "There was no one else at the corner other than Shoemaker and Mom."

"No one else was reported, but none of our witnesses saw anything until after the shooting, so could there have been another person who ducked inside the restaurant, or quickly or quietly walked away? Not likely; just thinking out loud," he said. "So, what if the target was your mother, why shoot Shoemaker?"

"Because he was standing in front of her?" Carla suggested. "Not exactly professional behavior. If he waits a few seconds, they would be separated as they crossed the street and he has a clear shot at her."

"Or he determines if he shoots the guy and he falls, he can then shoot the woman—make it look like a random shooting from a late-model car with the license plate 2BOOBS. The police aren't looking for a targeted killing, but instead some drugged or gang-related random shooting."

"That still doesn't explain the hit and run," Mike said.

"No it doesn't," Andrew stated.

"But you have an idea?" Carla stated.

"Not a good one, but maybe the shooter planned on hitting the first target, quickly followed my hitting the actual target, but realized there were witnesses and time suddenly became his greatest enemy, so he made a quick and erroneous calculation that by hitting them both with the car, he would take out the old lady who he had been sent to kill." When Mike and Carla just looked at him, he added, "Or he didn't see her behind his victim until after he shot, so he was taking out his most likely witness with his target."

"I like that scenario better," Carla said. "Why would anyone put a hit out on my mother? She's a Bible teacher who has nothing illegal or shady in her past. She's just a mother, a grandmother, a friend. She never had a classified job or a dangerous secret."

"That you know of," Andrew said.

"What?" Carla looked angry at him now.

"Okay," he conceded, "but a secret by definition means other people don't know about it. There doesn't seem to be a reason that Sandy would be the target. I said we were just brainstorming."

"I like brainstorming," Will said from the doorway, holding a cup of coffee.

"Come on in," Mike said. "Do you have any new revelations?"

"On which case?" he asked.

"Any of them," Carla said with exasperation.

"It's not really a revelation, but I had the idea to check into the driver who was killed with Adam's father. It seems he was involved in an accidental hit and run the year before he died. He lived in this small Georgia town in which his brother was the mayor."

"And he was a chauffeur?" Andrew asked.

"It's family," Will said. "What can I say. Anyway, a young woman was killed and her daughter was injured, but the chauffeur was never accused of a crime. It was ruled an accident and no charges were ever filed."

"So, the driver might have been the target?" Mike said.

"Could be," Will replied. "If he was, it was clever to take him out with a public figure. No one would suspect the driver to be the intended victim."

"What was the driver's name?" Andrew asked.

"Agustus Winters," Will answered. "He had been Adam's father's chauffeur for decades. The old guy probably did hit the woman and child by accident. But the fact that no charges were filed, could have pissed someone off."

Carla sat up straighter in her chair. "Winters? This wouldn't by chance be the small town of Harpton, Georgia, would it?"

"One and the same," Will said. "Have you been there?"

"No, but I talked to someone from there recently," she answered. "There is a young woman who has gone missing that I was asked to look into."

"You didn't say anything to us about her?" Andrew asked.

"She talked about becoming a forensic lab tech and wanted to work for us when she finished school. A mutual friend called to say she hadn't been able to get in touch with Taylor, so I located a friend of hers at the college who said the same thing. Taylor seems to be off everyone's radar. The college friend is named Roxanne Winters from Harpton, Georgia. Just how corrupt is this town?"

"Coincidence?" Mike asked. "How would Taylor's disappearance have any connection to an old hit and run or a murder?"

"It might not," Will said, "The town has only about 7500 people living there, and I'd bet close to half of them are related to a Winters. The family has been influential for generations."

"Again," Adrew said, "You didn't mention her disappearance to us?"

"We have so many open cases," Carla defended, "and Taylor is a bit quirky. I determined for now that she was probably off the grid intentionally; probably with some guy."

"Fair enough," Andrew replied, "but send me what you have on her anyway. It can't hurt to look into her and the Harpton factor."

Suddenly, Ben walked up next to Will. "Was there a company meeting I wasn't called to?" he asked.

"Just an impromptu brainstorming," Carla said. "You on your way home?"

"I was, but I love brainstorming," he replied.

Carla looked at her watch. "Maybe we'll continue this in the morning. Mike and I have to go or we'll be late for dinner with friends. The rest of you go home and get a good night's sleep. Tomorrow is another day and just might bring us a breakthrough on one of these cases."

"I also have dinner plans," Will stated, finishing the last of the coffee in his cup. "See you all in the morning."

When Carla and Mike got to Dolley's everyone else was already there.

"Sorry we're late," Carla said, as she walked across the room to kiss her mother's forehead. "How are you feeling?"

"I'm fine," Sandy said, "Any news from your end of the investigation?"

"Nothing concrete," she replied. "We were just in an impromptu staff meeting discussing how many dead ends we have seemingly investigated."

"Nothing that could be promising?" Dolley asked.

"Not yet," Carla said. "I'm hungry."

Everyone in the room was a bit suspicious concerning her quick reply.

Chapter 22

Marty and Diana spent a glorious week on the coast of Malta. It was a beautiful and romantic vacation that ended in a marriage proposal. Diana came back to the United States sporting a big smile and a huge diamond ring. However, it wasn't long before she voiced to Marty that she missed having friends and things to do.

"You mentioned that before our trip, my love," he said, as they sat together on the back porch in parkas and boots, with cups of steaming cocoa before a blazing fire. "I have to admit as cute as you look right now, I miss looking at you stretched out on white sand with no tan lines."

"It was freeing to just be me," she said.

"With no tan lines," he smiled.

Diana lifted his hand to her lips and kissed it. "You have given me everything," she said. "I believe God brought you into my life to help me walk away from my past."

"I'm not sure about God," Marty said, "but I have an offer for you if you are willing. Maybe it is another God thing, as you like to call the events in your life."

"Tell me," she said, with a smile of expectation.

"I know of a little girl who needs a mentor and I think you could be the perfect answer to her need."

"You mean a tutor?" Diana asked.

"No," he said. "She has a tutor. She doesn't have a mother or a big sister to show her how to do life and how to grow up to be confident like you."

"You see me as confident?" she asked.

"Of course," he said. "I have known and dated needy woman in my past. This little girl doesn't need someone with a lot of baggage. She needs someone like you who is open and honest."

"I don't know, Marty," Diana said. "I'm not sure I'd know how to mentor a little girl."

"Just meet her," he said. "I will introduce you as a friend of mine."

"A friend?" she asked, holding up her left hand with the engagement ring.

Marty chuckled. "Okay. I will introduce you as my fiancé. The point is you can spend some time with her and decide if you want to accept my offer. She will come for a visit with her nanny and her tutor."

"Who is she?" Diana asked.

"She is a relative of mine. I was close to her mother who died. She is a resilient little girl with a smile like yours. I just thought since she is coming here, you might consider having a role in her life."

"Of course. I would desire to know any relative of yours," Diana said. "When does she arrive?"

"In two days," he smiled. "However, I have to leave tomorrow on a business trip."

"The trip that cut our time in paradise short," she stated.

"Paradise is wherever we are together," he said, lifting her hand and kissing the finger with the ring. "I love that we will be together forever. There will be many more trips over the years, Diana."

"I have never been so happy," she said.

"We should have an engagement party!" Marty declared. "We'll plan it together when I get back. I want the world to know you are mine and I am yours."

Marty's business trip only took him to his small condo/office in Denver. He had a lot of loose ends to take care of and Diana didn't need to know he was only an hour away. He looked up from his desk as Marsha Barclay walked into his office.

"Really?" she asked. "A trip to Malta when we have so much going on here?"

"How do you know I was in Malta?" he asked.

"There is nothing I don't know," she replied. "And I'm tired of screwups. I thought you were only working with professionals now. That mess at the beach was unnecessary."

"The guy got in and out clean," he said.

"Yeah, but he antagonized that group we tangled with before. You know I don't care about the past. I don't like it when past issues raise their ugly heads after I have delegated them to just that."

"To just what?" he asked.

"The past, you numbskull."

"There's no need for name calling," he quietly said. "This isn't like you to be emotional."

"Screw you," she said, as she turned to leave. "Do what needs to be done, but I want minimal collateral damage. Got that?"

"Got it," he said to no one. Marsha's heels could be heard clicking down the long tile hallway to the elevators. "She could have said that on the phone," he mumbled, as he got back to his computer screen of shipping times and places."

The group they had tangled with sat around the conference desk in Mike and Carla's office. Not only was the staff gathered, but Longstreet, Mac, and Rob were also present.

"I just got back from Quantico," Rob announced. "DJ said they have made a connection between Justin Shoemaker and the illegal shipping ventures that cannot be connected to Marsha Barclay."

"How do you have a connection that cannot be connected?" Will asked.

"It's a government thing," Rob replied.

"We couldn't find any connection," Andrew said.

"They have files we aren't privy to," Mike said. "What did DJ tell you?" he asked Rob. "Shoemaker was nothing but another small-town nobody."

"But he wasn't," Rob stated. "According to DJ's guys, he was an informant for the FBI. He had once been on the payroll of some guy in Colorado who also can't be directly connected to Barclay, but who runs shipping internationally."

"Name?" Longstreet asked.

"We don't have one," Rob said.

"Do they?" Andrew asked.

"If they do, they aren't giving it out yet."

"So, how does this help us?" Carla asked.

"It doesn't seem like he was a hitman," Rob said.

"So why did he have my card?" Longstreet asked. "If DJ didn't know him, who would have given it to him?"

The group saw the lightbulb go on for Longstreet.

"Who has your cards?" Mac asked.

"Very few people," he said. "I'll have to get back to you on that."

Without any explanation, Longstreet got up and left the building. A minute later, Rob got a text that read I'll be out of town. Stay near Sandy.

"Longstreet?" Mac asked, as Rob looked at his phone.

"He's leaving town," Rob said.

"Should Sandy stay with us?" Mac asked.

"I'll stay at Longstreet's," Rob said.

"Put Ike at my mother's at night," Carla told him, and he nodded.

"How do we find this Colorado guy?" Mike asked his team.

"Do we have shipping logs that are questionable?" Andrew asked.

"We might from the past," Mike said, "but I don't know if those would be relevant to today."

"It might be a place to start," Andrew said.

"How about if you were to review billing statements for names that have recently been added as persons of interest," Mac asked.

"I can do that," Andrew said.

"I was wondering," Ben said, "If it would be possible for me to examine the forensic material from Adam's father's accident.

Do we know if there still is any and where it would be kept? It might help us connect dots to the Taylor case."

"What Taylor case?" Rob asked.

"Taylor is missing," Carla informed him.

"You said she wasn't answering her cell," he said, "You never told me she was a missing person in a case."

"We don't know that she is," Carla said. "She might be off the grid intentionally. You probably knew Taylor better than any of us. Would she just take off without telling her friends anything?"

Rob thought for a minute, "It's possible, but it's suspicious that she didn't tell Olivia anything."

"Olivia's the one that called me concerned. She said the same thing."

"How do you think she connects to another case?" Rob asked Ben.

"We have this murder case in which the chauffeur was killed with the public figure. We think there is a chance that the chauffeur might have been the target, although the police never considered him. His name was Agustus Winters, brother of the mayor of a small town in Georgia."

"How does this relate to Taylor?" Rob asked.

"Taylor's friend at school who also was concerned that she couldn't reach Taylor is from the same town. Her name is Roxanne Winters."

"What did she say?" Rob asked.

"She hasn't returned my calls this week," Carla said.

The meeting ended shortly after more discussion with everyone going different directions after being assigned different tasks.

Carla sat at her desk wondering if they were getting any closer anywhere. It felt like they just kept finding more wheels to spin.

Chapter 23

Sandy was getting crabby about being put under a watchful eye again. Carla suspected her headaches were worse than she let on, so she stopped by on her way home from work on Thursday. She walked in Sandy's house without knocking and asked why the door wasn't locked. The simple question sent her usually calm mother into a rage. Carla ducked as the dog toy her mother had just picked up on the floor flew past her head.

"Why don't you just have Laurie lock me up. No one could go after me in jail. Not a county prison or anything; just a nice local jail cell surrounded by police with three meals a day!"

"Mom," Carla said firmly, "Settle down. It was a simple question."

"No!"

"What?"

"I said no! I don't want to settle down. I need to get out of this house. I need to go for a walk with Allen and the dogs on the beach. I need to bake a cake and have someone around to eat it. I need to go to church or eat in a public restaurant, but settling down is not what I need. If I get anymore settled, I might as well go to sleep and not wake up."

Carla didn't know what to say, so she merely walked across the room and wrapped her arms around her mother, who broke into heartfelt sobs.

"I'm so sorry," she cried, "What is wrong with me?"

"Go wash your face and change your top," Carla said. "You and I are going to Taproom—no guards, no security, no men. We are going to have a girls night out—just the two of us."

"I'd like that," Sandy smiled. "We're not taking Ike, are we?"

"No," Carla smiled back at her, "we are not taking Ike."

When she pulled her phone from her pocket, Sandy looked skeptically at her.

"I'm just letting Mike know I don't know how late I'll be out so he doesn't worry about me."

"Men!" Sandy huffed, as she walked into the bathroom and closed the door.

Sandy not only washed her face and changed her top, a half hour later, she immerged in a pair of skinny jeans, a cute fitted sweater, sexy boots, and wearing more makeup than Carla had seen on her in months.

"Let's go attract some guys," she said, as she grabbed her purse off the counter.

"I'm married," Carla said.

"Too bad for you," Sandy quipped as she walked out the door.

Carla chuckled as she picked up her backpack and slung it over her shoulder. She had already checked her weapons, both the one under her sweater and the one at her ankle. She had also let Rob and Mike know where they were going. She ruffled Hero's fur and told him they'd be back later, then hurried to catch up to her freed-from-custody mother.

Taproom was busy. Carla and Sandy had to wait for a table, so they walked to the bar, ordered drinks and chatted with Chip.

"Still working two jobs with a baby at home?" Carla asked him.

"I'm working two jobs because there is a baby at home," he smiled.

"That's not nice," Sandy told him.

"I was only kidding," Chip assured her. "You look lovely tonight, Sandy."

"And I don't?" Carla teased.

"You always look lovely," Chip smiled.

"And I don't?" Sandy asked.

"I think I'm needed at the other end of the bar where I can get my foot out of my mouth.

"What did he say now?" Barb asked. "It's hard to get good help anymore."

She then gave Sandy a big hug. "I've missed you and I've missed Bible study. Are you going to be teaching us again?" Barb asked.

"I'm not 100% yet," Sandy said. "What happened to your wrist?"

"I broke it," she said. "It seems once the cast is off I'll have to go to therapy."

"What happened?" Carla asked, noticing Barb's bruised cheek.

"I fell into a wall. I worry about my kids falling and then I'm the one to fall."

"Oh, you poor thing," Sandy said. "How is everything else going? Have you had any help with the kids?"

"Marti has been a big help," she said, "and of course, Jake has been able to help if Rose or Elsa couldn't assist with kid care."

"You are at a busy time of life," Sandy said. "I remember those days. The years may go by quickly, but some days last forever."

"That's why I need Bible study to start up again as soon as you're ready, Sandy," she said, as Tap came out of the kitchen and she hurried off to wait a table.

"Hey Sandy, Carla," are you waiting to be seated?"

"Nice to be busy," Carla said. "Is Barb doing okay?"

"Your guess is as good as mine," he answered. "She avoids me these days, which I don't take as a good sign. I warned her about taking Jake back in, and I would never say 'I told you so,' but my guess is that it's not going well."

"Her broken wrist?" Carla asked.

"I'm sure you got the same story I did. It seems to be a rehearsed speech to anyone who asks."

"Well, as a server," Sandy said, "She would have to answer that question all day long."

Tap and Carla shared a smile that said 'always the positive one.'

Sandy and Carla had a nice evening. They had a wine before dinner and one with dinner. Several people they knew greeted them. A few gave condolences about Dash. Carla saw Will and Bella leave together. Neither of them saw her.

As they later walked out of Taproom, Carla looked both ways and smiled when she spotted Mike's car. She knew he would alert Rob that we were on the way home.

In the car, Sandy seemed unusually quiet.

"Everything alright?" Carla asked.

"I am reflecting," her mother said. "Talking to Barb, I realized how self-absorbed I've been lately."

"Mom, you've had a lot to deal with. Give yourself a break."

"That's the thing," she said. "I've dealt with big hurts or losses before and I didn't need a break. My behavior hasn't been a good reflection on my faith. I'm sorry I threw a dog bone at you."

Carla laughed. "I was a little surprised, but you missed."

"Only because you ducked," her mother smiled. "My aim was right on."

"You're right. I would have been clunked in the head if my reaction time had been slower. It's good training. You never know when an unforeseen dog bone will be hurled at you."

Sandy laughed, and then sobered. "Why has all of this been so hard on me this time?"

"Like I said, you've had a lot to deal with. I'm not an expert, but loss is one thing—an unknown terror is something else. And then Longstreet being a jerk didn't help."

"Was it him or me?" she asked. "Maybe I was putting unreasonable expectations on him. He was just doing his job."

"He could have done his job and been a friend at the same time," Carla said. "Tossing in an occasional flirtation would confuse anyone, even without the other stuff in your life."

"You think?"

"I know," Carla encouraged. "Barb asked about starting up Bible study again. Do you think you're up to it?"

"I'd like to be, but I'm not sure how much concentration I have with these headaches. They never go away, and I seem to be getting crazier as time goes on. You might have to announce yourself before entering in the future. Who knows what else I might throw."

Carla was quiet for a minute. "I think you need to see a doctor about another brain scan."

"You think I'm crazy?" she laughed, "Like part of my brain is now missing?"

"No, but you did get your head slammed against a concrete sidewalk. I think having it checked out one more time can't hurt."

"Maybe," Sandy said, as they pulled into her driveway. When Carla turned off the engine, Sandy asked, "Did you alert Rob that I was on the way back?"

"Indirectly," Carla said.

"What does that mean?" Sandy asked, and then said, "Oh, never mind. I don't want to know."

Sandy walked to the house with her mother. She played with Hero as Sandy unlocked the door. Carla walked in and waited for the lights to be turned on. She asked to use the bathroom just to make sure everything was secure and Rob knew they were home. Sandy followed Carla to the door as she was ready to leave.

"Thank you for this evening," Sandy said. "I needed it."

"We should do it more," Carla said. "I enjoyed it, too. And here comes Ike."

"You ladies have a nice evening?" Rob smiled.

"We did," Carla said. "Heard from Longstreet?"

"He'll be back tomorrow," Rob said.

"Tell him to give me a call," Carla told him.

"I'm sure he will."

Carla kissed her mom goodbye, and walked to her car thinking Longstreet must have news for them. She heard it in Rob's response.

Chapter 24

It was Friday evening. Diana had spent two days with little Emma and found her to be delightful. She not only occupied Diana's lonely days, but she brought out a maternal instinct in Diana that she never knew existed. In fact, she had always assumed she didn't have a maternal instinct, because her own mother had been so horrible. She did not have one memory of laughing or being love or even hugged as a child. The one time she went to counseling, the therapist suggested she had no memory of her father, who lived with them, because the memories were too hard to face. She had decided if that was the case, then counseling was definitely not a good idea. Her mother was usually high, which meant she operated in one of three modes—yelling, crying, or sleeping. She had learned to fend for herself or hide at an early age. Therefore, she reasoned, she'd have no idea how to be a good mother.

Emma was six years old and quite the chatterbox. After dinner, Rita, her nanny, was going to assist her with her bath, but Emma wanted Diana instead. Rita had told Diana that Emma was in a serious accident as a toddler and had multiple surgeries, but Diana was shocked to see her little legs. One was oddly shaped and they both had scars from multiple surgeries. Diana thought it was a miracle Emma walked as well as she did. Her gait was only thrown off when she was tired or when she ran.

As Rita ran the bath water, Emma asked when Papa Mark would be home. When Diana gave Rita a questioning look, she explained out of earshot that when Emma was little she couldn't say Marty. At first she just called him Mark, but at some point she added the Papa prefix.

"The poor little thing," Rita said, "she doesn't remember her mother and she never knew her father. He never cared to be part of her life. Dr. Martin stepped in as a relative and took over her financial care. He would stop in to see her a few times a year, always bringing candy and toys."

That realization just made Diana love him more.

By the time Emma's bath was over, Diana thought she could use dry pajamas as much as Emma. She took her little charge to the kitchen for a glass of milk and two cookies, before tucking her into bed. At Emma's insistence, she read two small books before turning out the light. She started to kiss Emma's forehead, but then didn't know if that would be appropriate, so she wished her a good night, and closed the bedroom door almost all the way as she had been instructed.

She turned to see Marty coming up the stairs. He put his finger in front of his lips, and motioned her toward the bedroom.

After closing the door, Diana jumped into his arms.

"I've missed you," she said.

He wrapped his arms around her and kissed her, realizing he'd missed her, too. As he set her on the thick carpet, he asked, "What happened to you?"

"What do you mean?' she asked, her eyes big.

"You're all wet," he said.

"Oh, that," she smiled. "I gave Emma a bath."

"Did you get in with her?" he wanted to know.

"No, silly," she replied, "But evidently happy little girls love to splash in the bathtub. I practically had to mop the floor with towels."

"So, you like her?" he asked.

"How could anyone not?" Diana said. "To think her own father wasn't interested in her and then her mother died, and all the surgeries she had to endure alone."

"I believe she was surrounded by a very caring staff of medical specialists."

"It's not the same as family, I'm sure," Diana said. "Are you hungry?"

"Just for you," he smiled, and Diana at once melted at the desire she saw in his eyes.

"I could use some help getting out of these wet clothes," she smiled.

"It will be my pleasure," he said.

Chapter 25

Friday morning, Longstreet walked under the sign that read Longstreet Campbell Investigations and Forensic Lab. He carried a box of bakery treats and his own large coffee.

"Good to see you, Boss," Carla said, as he entered the lobby.

"Don't call me Boss," he said, which had become a long-standing joke between them.

"Want me to call a team meet …" Carla stopped talking to answer her phone. "Carla Campbell," she said.

"Ms. Campbell, this is Roxie Winters. I just got back from a ten-day cruise. It was my graduation present from my parents. I saw you called. Do you have news on Taylor?"

"We don't, Roxie," Carla said, "And I'm about to go into an important meeting. Can I call you back this afternoon?"

"Sure," Roxie said. "I'll be home. I'll leave a message to wake me if I'm napping."

"I appreciate that," Carla said. "I'll call later. Bye."

"Team meeting," Longstreet said.

It took a half hour for everyone to be available with their coffee and pastry at the long table in the conference room. Mike thanked them for taking an early morning break.

"Hey," Ben said, "These pastries are the best, and we're all ready for some good news. Your name is on my paycheck," he said to Longstreet. "It's nice to meet you in person."

"You two haven't met?" Carla questioned.

"We have now," Longstreet said. "I would like to start with you catching me up on where we are on each of the three main cases we are working on."

Mike walked to the large board that displayed names, pictures, lines, and notes coming from Carla's computer.

The top line showed locations where each case began. The next line had the names of the people involved; Drake Asher, Justin Shoemaker, Sandy Asher, Daniel Chesterton, Agustus Winters, and Taylor Reese. The rest of each column gave information that had been verified or it listed lingering questions.

In trying to tie Murrells Inlet to the Colorado people, the only connection was the killer's Colorado driver's license that had been found at his vacated motel room. The other definitive link had been Longstreet's card on the body that knocked Sandy to the ground. Mike decided to start with that since Longstreet was present.

"Did you discover how Shoemaker got your card?" he asked his partner.

"It was as I suspected," Longstreet said. "I went to Quantico, where Melissa Freeman now lives in a condo near her grandchildren. She verified that she had given my card to our victim, and was truly sorry to hear of his death. She was able to enlighten me to their connection.

"It seems that a man we have been aware of for years named Clark Creek, had contacted Mr. Shoemaker about getting paid a great deal of money to kill Robert Armstrong, a former Special Forces friend of ours. The only place Mr. Creek knew to find Rob was at my beach house, where he sometimes stays when he is in the States.

"It seems that Justin Shoemaker was a legitimate businessman, but his twin brother Jordon Shoemaker is not. When Justin realized he had been mistaken for his brother, he played along, afraid of what might happen to him if he didn't. Then when he got home, he contacted the FBI office in Colorado. His family was moved out of harm's way, and Justin was put in touch with Melissa, who has a great deal of experience with … well, she has a great deal of experience.

"Melissa claims she did not give Justin my card, but she did have a couple on her desk when she met with him. She does not know why he was coming to see me or if he mistakenly thought he should warn Rob. His family is still in hiding and his brother has disappeared."

"Is it possible," Ben asked, "that it was Jordon Shoemaker carrying his brother's ID in case he got caught. Could he have heard about the mix-up and wanted the money offered to Justin?"

"It is," Longstreet said. "Until we find one of them, we can't be sure."

"Of course we can," Ben said. "Most identical twins have almost identical DNA, but it is not exactly identical. However, even monozygotic twins, who are considered genetically identical because they came from one ovum, or egg, can be differentiated, not by general forensic testing, but by a test that melts down their DNA and in a matter of hours they could be told apart. Also, their fingerprints were the same at conception, but as the baby develops within the womb, their fingerprints change ever so slightly as they grow.'

"Can you do this test?" Carla asked.

"No, but I'm sure Quantico could, however, we'd have to have something to compare for either the DNA or the fingerprint testing."

"I'm sure that could be arranged," Longstreet said. "I'll have Melissa contact CBI for samples from Jordon."

"If the bad brother was posing as the good brother, they should know that too. The good brother's family could be in danger," Andrew commented.

"So, how does this help us identify the shooter who followed up with a hit and run? Was he after the good brother or the bad brother?" Will asked.

"And is there a connection between Clark Creek and anyone else on our board?" Mike asked.

Carla kept typing on her laptop, and more questions appeared on the large, white board in front of them.

Longstreet shrugged and said, "What about the columns further to the right? What do we know?"

Andrew spoke up. "We haven't found anything suspicious concerning Adam's father, Daniel Chesterton, however, the friend who supposedly called to meet him was located yesterday. Gutherie Williams is a John Doe that has been in the Atlanta morgue."

"Did he die after Daniel? Mike asked.

"No," Andrew said, "which seems to imply that the call to meet him in Mechanicsville was a hoax, further making it seem that Daniel was not involved in nefarious dealings."

"So, we think his chauffeur was the target?" Will asked.

"That's the trail I'd follow," Andrew suggested. "I know we just talked about the good brother and the bad brother in Colorado, but in the case of the Winter's brothers in Harpton, Georgia, they might both be bad. Maybe the chauffeur has been feeding information he knows or even just hears about in the car to his family."

"Like in the movie Sabrina," Will stated.

"What?" Andrew asked.

"The chauffeur listened for comments about stocks made in the backseat of the limo and invested, accumulating a fortune."

No one spoke, so Mike continued. "Let's go to the last column. Carla just got a call before our meeting from Roxie Winters, Taylor's friend. She's to call Roxie back this afternoon. If the family is corrupt, could it have something to do with Taylor's disappearance. Could she have overheard something that got her killed?"

"How do you get answers out of the friend without spooking her if she does know something about her family's involvement in Taylor's disappearance or even just knows about family business?" Ben asked.

"I'm wondering if I should talk to her in person?" Carla said.

"If she does know something, wouldn't that make her more suspicious? Plus, she might alert family members that she's being interrogated," Mike said. "A phone call still makes your questions about Taylor and not Roxie or her family."

"Okay, but I need to find out how she is related to Agustus," Carla said. "I'll think of something before I call her back."

"So, what are our new assignments?" Andrew asked.

"Longstreet will contact Melissa concerning the CBI and getting hair or something to determine DNA. She'll also alert them that the wrong brother might be dead. Maybe the bad brother has a record and has been fingerprinted," Mike added.

"I'll make the call," Longstreet said. "I'll also give DJ a heads up that we're going to have his buddy in forensics do that special DNA test when we get the samples. If he has any questions, I'll have him call Ben."

"He'll know the test," Ben said. "If you get fingerprints, I can compare those for you."

"What have you found on our mysterious Doc Martin?" Will asked Carla.

"I have looked everywhere for a Dr. Martin that might fit the profile, but continue to come up empty. Anyone else who wants to go down that rabbit hole is welcome to try," she said. "And I'll let you all know what I find out from Roxie this afternoon."

"Andrew," Mike said, "I want you to research this Gunthrie Williams, the John Doe. Find out why no one knew who he was, and if you can find a connection between him and our chauffeur Agustus."

"On it," Andrew replied.

"Anything I can do?" Will asked.

"It's not legal work," Carla said, "but you could call hospitals around both the Savannah area where Taylor went to school and the Harpton/Atlanta area where Roxie's family resides. See if they have any Jane Does matching Taylor's description. I'll email you her photo. I think it's time to worry that she just didn't take off with some guy, which has been my hope. I'm still praying that's the case."

"I'm not as good as Carla at snooping," Mike said, "but I'll see if I can find a connection anywhere to Clark Creek or Marsha Barclay.

Chapter 26

The night of the engagement party was snowy and cold, but inside the fires were going and everyone was in good spirits. When Marty announced their engagement to unsuspecting guests, there was a round of applause as the bottles of champagne were popped open. Diana looked amazingly beautiful and radiated happiness, as did Marty.

After dinner, as the music was starting, a woman Diana recognized from previous parties, came up to her with a less-than-sincere smile.

"Congratulations," she said. "You know you aren't the first fiancé we have toasted, don't you?"

When Diana didn't respond, she continued, "I was in your place once; well, not as a fiancé, but as a girlfriend. Has he loaned you to his buddies yet? Once the newness of your relationship wears off, he will. It's a nice ring, though," she added before slipping back through those on the dance floor.

As Diana reeled from the woman's innuendos, she looked up to see Marty walking toward her with his glowing smile. She decided to believe the woman was a jealous bitch, and trust the love of her life to be who she knew him to be. She returned his smile, as he took her hand and led her to the dance floor.

"I love you," he whispered in her ear, as they began to move with the music. "I love you as I've never loved before."

The evening continued with Marty at her side. After midnight, he disappeared, as he usually did. Still not feeling like anyone in the room was really her friend, she walked to a quiet corner away from the noise and people and looked out at the snow.

"It's beautiful, isn't it," a deep voice said over her shoulder.

When she gave a startled response, he chuckled and added, "But not as beautiful as you are."

He then put his arm around her waist, and pulled her back against him as he kissed her neck and his free hand began to roam. Reaching back, she pulled his hair as hard as she could. The action surprised him, causing his grip on her to lessen enough for her to turn and slap him.

"How dare you!" she exclaimed, expecting him to be angry, but instead, Greg laughed and reached for her again. "Marty said you were feisty," he smiled. "I also like that in a woman."

"Don't touch me!" She spit out the words as her eyes glared at him. "You'll be sorry you did that."

"Are you threatening me?" His smile was gone. "Don't think you're the first to sport a ring, and you won't be the last. When the shine is gone, I'll have you. I hate to tell you, Babe, but he needs me more than he needs you."

Diana was still shaking when she saw Marty looking for her. She hurried to him, wrapping her arms around his waist and looking up in worried eyes.

"Is everything okay?" he asked.

"Fine," she smiled, "I'm just getting tired of people. When will this party be over?"

"Soon," he chuckled, and looked toward the door. "I think the snow will get people moving. They like my parties, but no one wants to get stuck up here. Let's go tell our guests good-night."

"Can you tell them?" she asked, seeing Greg as one of the guests by the door. "I'm not feeling well. I'd like to go on upstairs."

"Are you sure you're okay?" His smile faded.

"I'm fine, Darling," she said. "I'll be waiting for you upstairs."

"I'll be up as soon as possible," he told her, turning to empty the rooms as quickly as etiquette allowed.

It was nearly an hour before Marty walked into their bedroom, expecting to see Diana in bed, he was surprised to see her pacing the room.

"Greg attacked me," she said, as soon as he closed the bedroom door.

"What?"

"You heard me," she said.

"When?"

"While you were out of the room doing whatever it is you do when you leave me alone with those people," she said. "What is it that you do?"

"Nothing that concerns you," he sighed, as he removed his jacket and put in on a hanger.

"So, you don't care that Greg assaulted me?" she asked.

"Of course, I care," he said as he walked to her, "I'll speak to him about it. That ring on your finger should have said 'hands off'."

"One of our guests," she said, emphasizing the last word, "told me that I should expect you to pass me around to your friends in the future. Is that true?"

"Diana," he sighed, bending his head to kiss her before she pulled away from him. As she returned to pacing, he said. "I told you that you are not the same as the others. I love you. I want you to become my wife one day and for us to live to be old together."

"If I ask you a question, will you tell me the truth?" she asked.

"I never lie to you," he lied.

"Were you engaged before?"

"Yes."

"More than once?"

"Yes."

"Have you been married?"

"No."

"Did you allow your friends to sleep with your other fiancés?"

"Diana," he sighed, as he began to undress near the closet. "I told you there have been others, but I also told you it is different with you. We have something that I've never experienced with any one before. Why can't you believe that? Have I behaved in any way that suggests I am not who I say I am? If you want me to ban Greg from future parties, I will."

"I do," she said.

"Okay."

"I don't get it," she said. "Why aren't you as angry at Greg as I am?"

"He's a fool," Marty said. "He should have known better, but he only knows me, and I told you I'm not a nice guy. If he could know you and how I feel about you, he would have been more respectful."

Diana walked to him. "Will you really not invite him to future parties?" she asked.

"He's off the invitation list as of now," he smiled, cupping her chin and lowering his mouth to hers. "No one is more important to me than you. I'm sorry Greg misbehaved."

"What about the others?" she asked.

"You want me to eliminate all men from our guest list?"

"No," she said, "what about the other fiancés? Did you offer them to your buddies, as that woman said?"

"I can guess who said that to you," he said, as he continued to strip off his clothes and put on a robe. "It was not like I gave those women to my friends; they went on their own accord."

"I don't believe you," she said.

"Honey, Greg has never had a girlfriend. Every time I invite him to a party I pay for his date. Usually, I do the same for Jeff Morgan."

"You pay for hookers for them?"

"Escorts," he corrected, "beautiful and expensive escorts. Both Greg and Jeff have more money than sense. Those girls not only get paid by the agency, but are generously paid by their dates for their willingness to please. I used to be more like them, only I never used drugs as they do. Greg was probably high when he approached you."

"I don't believe that," she said, putting her hand on his chest.

"Which part?" he asked.

"That you were ever like Greg. He's a snake and I'm a little hurt that you aren't upset with him."

"I told you I'd ban him from future parties," Marty told her. "You never have to see him again. Now can we go to bed? Let me wipe any thoughts of Greg or any other man from that beautiful mind of yours. By the way," he said, before kissing her, "I never had a woman who interested me beyond her physical attributes. It's different with you, Diana. I love everything about you, and it just might be the death of me."

As she melted against him, he leaned down and put his arm behind her knees to gently lift her to his bed. He wondered as he did if that last statement might be more correct than he wanted to consider.

Chapter 27

Everyone took a much-needed break from the investigations for Christmas. Mike, Carla and Sandy flew to Nashville to spend two days at Mitch and Beth's lovely home. Julie and Chris were there, also. It had been six years since Sandy had spent a Christmas with just her family in Nashville. Billy had been a part of that Christmas, and the memories flooded her with emotion.

She remembered how he teased Connor and Riley who were little kids at the time, and how it had been a white Christmas. They had all gone outside to experience the unusually heavy snowfall, and Billy had assisted them in building both a snowman and a pile of snow with a hole dug in it that they called a snow fort.

She looked around the room and saw her life in her children. Mitch looked so much like Donny, who never got the chance to grow old or know his child. Carla had the coloring and the stubborn determination of her father, Carlos. Julie didn't look just like either of her parents. She was a combination of Sandy and Billy, and everyone's favorite, probably because she was the baby of the family. She did, however, have her father's laugh. Sandy guessed her siblings heard that in her also.

After the holidays, the people on the investigative team were again busy trying to keep anyone else from being killed. The rest of those at the beach were enjoying the cooler January weather. One afternoon, instead of just walking the dogs near the house, Sandy and Longstreet decided to walk them around Market Commons, and then eat outside with the two dogs quietly watching people pass by.

"I know there is still a threat out there," Sandy said, "But it feels like its over concerning me."

"I'll always keep you safe," he said.

"How are you going to do that living in the mountains?" she asked.

"I have ways," he smiled.

"I don't need a million cameras in my house and car. Are you going to make me wear a hat or a brooch with a camera in case I go anywhere alone?"

"I might just work on that," he smiled.

"You know what I'd like?" she asked.

"Tell me," he replied as the server refilled their water glasses.

"I'd like to see your mountain home."

"Why?" he asked, casually as he took a long drink of water.

"Because all these years I've tried to imagine what it is like. How can I picture you there if I can't see it in my mind's eye?"

"That's probably a workable plan some day," he said.

"That's a very vague response," she told him.

"Did you have a specific date in mind?" he asked.

"No."

"Then how am I supposed to have a specific answer?"

"Forget it," she said, "You're impossible."

"What did I say?"

"Really?" she stopped with a French fry halfway to her mouth. "Are you going to play dumb?"

"I can be kind of dumb sometimes," he said. "I'm not getting any younger. Ike and I were content doing nothing in the mountains day in and day out."

"Now, why don't I believe that?"

"I don't know," he said, "you should."

"Then you were forced to come live in that little beach house and babysit me and Hero," she said. "No one is making you stay. You're free to go back to doing nothing day in and day out."

Longstreet chuckled. "You're cute."

"I'm cute?" she said. "You like annoying me, don't you?"

"Sometimes, but it's only because I like you. It's the same reason I pulled Jenny Johnson's ponytails in the fourth grade and the same reason I snap at Carla when she calls me Boss."

"So, you're the emotional age of an eight-year-old?"

"My ex-wife would probably think that was being generous."

"How did a handsome, sexy, emotionally impaired guy like you go all these decades without getting married again. There must have been dozens of willing women."

"I think they thought I had the emotional maturity of an eight-year-old

"No, really," she said. "I'm asking you seriously."

"I guess I failed so miserably the one time I tried to be a family man that I chose not to risk failure again. Instead, I spent my life doing things I was good at, not the one thing I failed at. My ex-wife and son were lucky to have a good man come along and be what I couldn't be. He loves them and they both love and respect him. Not being respected was not a path I wanted to risk again."

"You were young and finding your own way," she said.

"Just an excuse," he replied. "Look at DJ. He was me or I was him. Anyway, he's making it work, and I see his reward. I didn't know how to do that. I don't think I have it in me to be a good husband, no matter how much I might have moments of missing what never can be."

"That sounds really insightful," she said.

"Thank you," he said.

"If I used the word 'bullshit' I'd use it now."

Longstreet choked on the water he was about to swallow.

"I'm going to the ladies' room," she said, as she stood. "I think the boys are ready to go back home."

After pulling his vehicle under his beach house, Longstreet let the dogs run around to Sandy's porch. As he and Sandy each closed their car doors, they heard Ike growling.

"Stay here," he commanded, pulling a weapon from a concealed holster.

With gun drawn, he walked around the back side of Sandy's house, where Hero looked anxious and Ike was focused on Sandy's back door. Stepping past the dogs, Longstreet went to put in the security code and realized the door was ajar. He quietly opened it and allowed Ike to step inside, head up and ears alert.

After he and his dog had cleared the house, he holstered his weapon and walked around to where Sandy sat in his locked car.

"All clear," he said, as he opened her door and took her hand to assist her in standing. He could see she was shaken.

"I thought we locked the door when we left," he said.

"I know I locked it," she said, wide-eyed.

"I walked through and it's clear," he said. "Come on. We'll walk through it together."

They did just that. While Sandy was upstairs, Longstreet looked through things like the refrigerator and pantry to see if anything had been touched. He called Carla and told her about the unlocked door. He suggested she send Henry to sweep the house. He hated to tell Sandy that he did that, but didn't see any way around it.

"Let's leave the dogs and go have a drink at Taproom," he said.

"Why?" she asked. "What's going to happen here while I'm gone? Hidden cameras?"

Longstreet laughed. "No," he said. "Mike's bringing a guy to sweep your house just in case we did lock the door. Maybe Dolley stopped by and forgot to lock up. Does she have your code? Could she have borrowed sugar?"

"She does have the code," Sandy brightened.

"Good," he said. "I'll call Mac from the car and see if they want to meet us at Taproom. We'll take your car. You can drive."

"Why?" she asked suspiciously.

"So, you don't feel like anyone is babysitting you," he said, draping an arm around her neck. "Lock up. We'll leave the boys on your porch.

Mac and Dolley came in ten minutes after Sandy and Longstreet. Dolley had a floral scarf tied around her head the way the young boys tie bandanas around theirs.

"Is this a new fashion statement you're trying?" Sandy asked.

"My hair was a mess and I didn't have time to fix it," she said. "I learned this from Maggie Mason after her bout with chemo. I think it just might catch on."

"With who?" Sandy laughed.

"Old ladies having a bad hair day," she shrugged. "Anyway, we're here. It's been a while since the four of us were together. I was commenting on the way over that we should have a card night soon."

"I'd like that," Sandy said. "But before we order, I have a question. Did you by any chance go by my house today while we were out?"

"No," Dolley said, "Why?"

"We got home and the back door was unlocked and I was sure that I locked it as we left."

"I do that all the time," Dolley said. "Don't I make you go back and check the locks sometimes after we're already in the car?"

"She does," Mac said. "Even though there have only been a couple times that she thought it was locked and it wasn't."

"Well," Sandy sighed, "I guess it's possible I locked it yesterday and remembered it at today."

"Are you worried?" Dolley asked.

"Oh," she said, "I want to get over being anxious, but stupid stuff like this keeps popping up."

"What other things have you noticed?" Mac asked, after a quick glance at Longstreet.

"Yesterday, when I went to brush my teeth, there was hardly any toothpaste left in the tube, and I was sure it was almost full the morning before. I'm going tomorrow for another brain scan of some sort. It's all probably from that bump on the head."

"I wish I had a reason to get a brain scan," Dolley said.

"You say some strange things, Dolley," Mac told her.

"I know!" she declared. "That's why I'd like a brain scan. I'd like to know if I'm not all there."

The other three at the table laughed.

"This is a very noisy table," Laurie Baker said, as he and Marti walked up to say hello.

"Are you two coming or going?" Dolley asked.

"We just got here," Marti said. "I've been out of town and Laurie has been working a lot of hours. We decided we'd take an evening and just chill."

"How's Barb doing?" Sandy asked.

"Not well," Marti said. "Jake is gone again, and I'm glad. It's hard on Josh when he keeps leaving."

"Keeps leaving?" Mac asked. "She told Dolley things were going well."

"She found an Asian lady who has been staying with the kids when I'm gone, so that's probably what's going well. He took her to the ER one night. She claimed she fell, but Jake was gone the next day for a week. When he came back, she let him move back in, but he left again this week, and I'm hoping she'll stick to her guns this time. I think seeing what it does to Josh is the biggest motivator not to let him keep using her."

"It's sad," Sandy said. "I always liked Jake."

"Jake's a decent guy when he's straight, but I've seen him a couple times when he seemed to be high. He probably means what he tells her when he's sober, but if he can't stay sober, then he needs to walk away."

"What about child support?" Sandy asked, "I'm sure it's hard raising two kids on what she makes. She doesn't need him walking away completely."

"I don't think he's been paying her," Marti said. "Maybe someday he'll get his act together, but right now he does more harm than good."

"I'll call her tomorrow," Dolley said. "Maybe there's a time we can get together and support her."

"That would be nice," Marti said. "I think she's embarrassed. She's kind of shut everyone out, but if Jake's gone, she'll need friends around."

As he was paying the check for dinner, Longstreet got a text from Mike that the house was good for now, but to call or stop by in the morning. Carla would be picking her mother up early to take her for her scans.

Longstreet arrived with pastries again. He left them in the conference room by the coffee and went to Mike's office.

Mike told him they didn't find any bugs in Sandy's house, but he also took Ben with a UV light to check for fingerprints.

"Fingerprints?" Longstreet asked.

"Yes, and Ben found an anomaly. There were a few places where it there were no fingerprints."

"Meaning?"

"Most cabinets and door handles had finger fingerprints, as they should."

"Sandy, Carla, me," Longstreet said there are many people who could have left fingerprints.

"That's true," Mike said. "That's why finding places like the medicine cabinet and the refrigerator door handle without any fingerprints seemed odd."

"Could it be she just cleaned those places?"

"It could, and Ben checked all the product in both places and found fingerprints on every bottle, box or container," Mike said. "I'm setting up with Lewis at True Omega Security to put additional cameras at her place. She's not going to like it, but it may keep her safe."

"Ike and I aren't going anywhere until this is all over," he said. "I need to be more diligent about setting the cameras during the times we walk the dogs and the house is completely available. Sandy was sure she locked the door. I didn't say anything, but I watched her do it. Someone was in her house while we were gone with the dogs yesterday.

"This is not good," Mike said. "We have to find who is behind it. The fact that they're still around should give us a shot. Should we take fingerprints?"

"I'm sure if they were wiped, it was probably the only place the intruder removed gloves for some reason," Longstreet said. "I'm glad Ben checked bottles and jars."

"He didn't check whose prints, just that there were some vs. being wiped off."

"Sandy is gone with Carla this morning," Longstreet said. "Why don't I take him back there now and we'll bring some things back here."

"She's not going to like it," Mike warned.

"If it keeps her alive, I don't care what she likes," he said. "I'll be the bad guy. You can let her get mad at me."

Sandy didn't get back from the hospital till after dark. For some reason, she was very nauseous after the tests. By evening, she was better. The nurse suggested she stay, but Sandy wanted to go home and sleep in her own bed.

She slept okay, but by noon the next day, she was ill again. When Ben heard that, he told Carla that she needed to go to the ER or she needed to let him take a blood test.

"What are you thinking?" Carla said.

"I had that crazy case last summer that ended up being thallium poisoning. When Bella was here that day, I was explaining to her that it was colorless, tasteless and odorless, but it can kill a person in a week. The symptoms mimic the flu. The stuff they gave your mother for her scan should not have made her sick like that."

"That's what the nurses kept saying yesterday. They said they had never had anyone so sick after a scan," Carla told him.

"Let's go," Ben said. "I can run the blood test faster than driving her there, checking her in and demanding they do a test they normally don't do."

"I'll drive," Carla said, "Get whatever you need."

When Ben and Carla entered the house, they could hear Sandy throwing up. Carla left Ben in the living room to find her mother. She was shocked when Sandy stood up and reached for a wash cloth to wipe her warm face.

"Why are you here?" she asked Carla.

"I brought Ben," she said. "He wants to take a blood test."

"They took one yesterday in the hospital," Sandy said. "You were there."

"Ben said it probably wasn't the right test," Carla explained.

"Honey, I'm so exhausted and just want to sleep," she said.

"It won't take but a minute," Carla said, "I'll help you get back in bed and Ben can take a little tube of blood in there. Will that be okay?"

"Why does he want to take it?" she asked.

"Just to be cautious," Carla said. "It will make me happy."

"Okay," Sandy said, leaning on Carla's arm as together they walked back to Sandy's bed.

Carla propped up the pillows and helped her mother into bed. Sandy wanted to lay down, but Carla encouraged her to sit up for just a few minutes. She smoothed out the blanket and called Ben, who came in. greeted Sandy and quickly got what he needed. He waited for her in the living room.

"I don't think she should be alone," Ben said. "Take me back to the lab and come back here. I'll call as soon as I know, but her breathing is very shallow. The symptoms can be almost non-existent and then come on quickly."

"You think she's been poisoned?" Carla asked, as she locked the door, and phoned Longstreet as they hurried to the car.

"Hey," he answered.

"You home?" she asked.

"Yeah, why?"

"Mom's still sick. Ben just took a blood sample. He suspects she might have been poisoned. Will you stay with her until I get back?"

"I'll go over now," he said.

Carla backed her car out of the drive. "She may not be happy to see you, but she may be sick enough she doesn't care."

"I can handle it," he said. "We'll keep in touch."

"I'll be back in thirty minutes or less."

"Drive safely. I'll be here."

Sandy did have thallium poisoning. Carla called an ambulance, knowing it would get her admitted faster than going in on her own through the ER. She gave the EMT's, one of which she knew, the blood vial and results from Ben's lab. By the time they got her to the hospital, her speech was slurred, she was drooling, and her breathing was very slow.

Longstreet had driven Carla behind the ambulance, and she called Mike on their way. When Mike walked into the waiting room, she walked into his arms and sobbed. Longstreet stood by helplessly. Dolley and Mac weren't far behind them.

Fortunately, the forensic lab's reputation accelerated the administration of the drug Prussian Blue, the antidote for thallium poisoning. However, Sandy's symptoms were still scary. The antidote is used to bind the thallium in the intestines to help it be eliminated instead of absorbed into the system. It is not a quick fix, but will continue to be given for days or even weeks until the body has eliminated all the radioactive poison.

Sandy slipped into a coma in the ambulance. She was quickly transferred to ICU upon arrival. The doctors told Carla it was now a waiting game. Longstreet called Detective Baker, who met them at the hospital. Dolley called Rose to notify Sandy's friends to be praying for her recovery. Longstreet left with Laurie Baker. He wasn't sure what to do, but he couldn't just pace the hospital corridor. That was not his nature to just wait. Someone had intentionally poisoned Sandy. Ben wanted everything eatable from her home, including her toothpaste. Longstreet wanted answers. Someone was responsible. Someone was going to pay.

Chapter 28

Sandy came out of the coma after four days, but she wasn't doing well. Her body was not getting rid of the thallium as quickly as they had hope. Carla had read up on the long-term effects of thallium and wished she hadn't. Between herself, Julie, and Mitch, Sandy was never alone. It was Julie's turn to spend the night, so Carla could get some sleep, but she couldn't sleep, so she got up, showered and got into the office early.

She made a pot of coffee, and while it was brewing, she wiped off the counter and checked the pantry to make a list of supplies that might be getting low. After writing only a couple things on her notepad, she poured a cup of coffee and walked back to her office. The forecast was for rain and the skies were gray. She flipped on a few lights as she passed the wall switches. Saturday's mail was sitting on the credenza in the entry room she referred to as the lobby. She grabbed it and entered her office.

As her computer booted up, she glanced at the mail, not seeing anything important enough to open this early. Taking a sip of her coffee, she opened her email and saw mail from DJ with the title: *Important! Doc!* Carla immediately put her coffee to the side and opened the email. The short message said that agents in Denver were set up to monitor info on a drug shipment and instead recorded this. Attached was a video. Carla started watching it, stopped it and called Mike.

"Forget something?" he asked good-naturedly. "What time did you leave?'

"Just a bit ago," she said. "Get in here right away."

"What's wrong?" he asked instantly on alert and grabbing his keys.

"I just got a video from Quantico. I haven't watched it all, but it looks like they have a lead on our doctor."

"On my way," he said.

Carla stopped the video, and walked back to the conference room to pour Mike a coffee. She tried to temper her expectations. The video was shot from across the street, so there was traffic noise and pedestrian interference that cut out some of the words, but even with the grainy picture, she recognized the woman as Marsha Barclay and was pretty sure the guy she was talking to was Clark Creek. He had on a denim jumpsuit and a ball cap, but at one point he turned his head enough to see his profile. She hadn't watched it all. His identity might become clearer before it ended.

Carla paced until Mike came through the door.

"What have we got?" he asked, as he walked directly to her office and took the coffee she handed him.

"I didn't want to watch it alone," she said.

"That important?" he asked, looking at her with raised eyebrows.

"It's just that I've been waiting for us to catch a break, and now that we might have, I didn't want to see it alone."

Mike put his hand on her shoulder as she sat at her desk and started the video from the beginning.

"The memo said the agents were waiting for information on a drug shipment and just got this conversation by luck," she said as it started.

After only a few seconds, Mike asked, "Is that Barclay?"

"Yep, and I think that's Clark Creek she's talking to." Together they listened.

"What are you saying?" Clark asked.

"Exactly what I just said," Marsha said without emotion. "Doc has to disappear."

"Why?"

"He's getting sloppy. "I don't trust him anymore."

"Because?

"He cut off Greg! Really? A man in love is dangerous. He talks too much and he gets too careful. I want them all to disappear."

"All?"

"Make it definitive and public. I need three bodies to be part of the carnage."

"Three?"

"Doc, the fiancé and the young girl."

"Why the girl?"

"No loose ends this time. I want charred bodies that are unrecognizable; no fingerprints or DNA to trace.

"He's not a liability."

"I'm telling you he is. It has to be a fire or an explosion. I want it done soon. Doc was useful, but it doesn't work anymore."

"What about Greg?"

"What about him?"

"Won't he be suspicious? Aren't you afraid of who he might talk to?"

"I think eliminating Doc will keep a lot of people quiet. If you can't do this, I'll find someone who will, but don't think you are indispensable," she said. "I've depended on you for a very long time, but I'm getting tired of messy situations, Clark."

"We both have accumulated enough to just walk away," he suggested.

"Retire?" she laughed. "And do what? Take up crocheting and golf? I don't think so. Just do your job. It's not like you haven't done this before. I know you don't like to get your hands dirty, but passing the dirty work off to underlings has cost us. Love's a bitch," she said. "It's ruined Doc and he needs to go. I'm counting on you."

Clark nodded.

"I'm leaving the country for a month," she said. "I expect the elimination of our problem to be completed when I return."

Mike and Carla looked at each other. They had just watched two people calmly discuss killing three people including a child. For a moment, neither of them spoke.

Mike texted Longstreet to come by the office, and then picked up the phone and dialed DJ.

"You saw the video," DJ said.

"Were they able to follow the persons of interest?" Mike asked him.

"They weren't *their* persons of interest." DJ said.

"But they had just witnessed the order for a hit on three people," Carla exclaimed.

"That's why they forwarded it to us. Colorado agents were chastised for not tracking at least Clark, and they are scrambling to alert all LEO's to the threat of a staged public assassination, but all we really have is a verification that Doc exists and he is in Colorado. It also seems there are possibly two innocent people who may go down with him."

"What's the plan?" Mike asked.

"Rob's here," DJ said. "The FBI is searching for opportunities. Do you guys know more than we do?"

"You've been kept up to date," Carla said.

"I can't say anymore," he said. "I'll send Rob back to you."

When DJ disconnected, Mike walked around the desk and neither spoke for a minute.

"Call Harvey to have our office swept again for bugs," he said. "Then when the team gets in, we need to update them."

Chapter 29

Marty promised Diana that the three of them would take his private jet to Reno, Nevada. He made plans for them to have a short, simple wedding ceremony in a field of lavender. Then they would fly to the Dominican Republic for a vacation. Diana and Emma were so excited. Marty was gone a lot every day, but he said he had a lot of things to take care of before they left. Diana had ordered white dresses for both her and Emma, and she had ordered a bunch of beach and vacation clothes for all of them. Every time the doorbell rang with another box or delivery, it was like Christmas.

Her wedding day finally arrived. Marty had been gone the entire day before, getting home tired and dirty after midnight.

The morning of her wedding, Diana was so excited she could hardly act like an adult. She wanted to run and laugh like sweet Emma. Marty had all their luggage taken to the plane, including wedding attire. He told the staff they would be gone for a month, and paid them generously, including Rita and Sharon, the tutor.

As excited as Diana was about the wedding, she was just as excited when they stepped into the small private plane. She had never experienced such luxury. She was told the flight was only two and a half hours to Reno, and was asked if she and Emma would like coffee or cocoa with their breakfast. Diana was almost too excited to eat, but she thought she should have something. After all, Marty had provided all these amazing details. No wonder he had been gone so much.

Marty sat across the plane with his coffee and watched his two girls. He had lived his life for his own benefit, too often taking a life that interfered with his plans. He regretted some of that, but it had allowed him to amass a not so small fortune. Now, he was done. He would marry the most lovely and charming woman he had ever known, who loved him for what she saw as good, and didn't even want to know about what he might have been. She told him one night that everyone had secrets. There were parts of her life where she had lied in order to survive. She didn't care who he used to be; she loved him for who he was.

Marty didn't know how he had been given this second chance. He had liquidated most of his holdings. A lawyer who had always been most discrete saw to the details. He knew there was a chance something from his past might catch up with him, so he had created a will that in the event of his death, everything he had would go to Diana and Emma. He had even managed in a week to have passports created in the names Diana Martin and Emma Martin. He had then purchased a small villa in the Dominican Republic where they could live, and Diana would not have to live in seclusion anymore. He would enjoy taking his girls out to eat and to the beaches and fresh markets. He had only been there once, but he had noticed immediately that the people were friendly and the pace of life was slower than it was state-side. When he was young, that had annoyed him. Now, he was looking forward to it.

Using the name Mark Jones, Marty had booked a fifteen-minute wedding, supposedly for friends. He had also made arrangements for a photographer who would take pictures and then give Marty the memory card with a flash drive of the pictures. He told Diana because the flight was long, he had planned a nice dinner on the plane. He promised her a wedding cake within a few days. Diana assured him she didn't need all those fancy things. Being his wife and a picture to look at over and over would be enough. He was determined to give her the world. The guy he used to be would have laughed at the guy he was now.

Their stop in Reno only lasted two hours. He was sorry in some ways, because it should have been more for Diana. She and Emma looked beautiful in their simple, white dresses. They went to the clerk office and for less than $100 dollars, they got a marriage license for Mark and Emma Martin. Then, they took a cab to the Lavender Ridge Wedding Park. The hosts welcomed the little wedding party, saying his friend Mark Jones had paid them very well to squeeze in their short ceremony between two already scheduled weddings. After saying their vows, a formal picture was taken inside, and then the photographer had followed them into the fields of gently blowing lavender with the mountains as a backdrop. He had taken a dozen of the bride and groom, a few of the 'family,' and then more of Diana and Emma with joy-filled faces skipping and laughing in the lavender field.

With both of them talking at once, he had shooed the girls into a cab that took them back to the private airstrip, where their new plane awaited. This one had a sleeping cabin in the back. Once they were in the air and had looked at the pictures a dozen times, Emma fell asleep in one of the cabin recliners. Marty and Diana slipped back to the room that was mostly bed and consummated their marriage as they happily glided through white clouds.

Chapter 30

Ben walked into Carla's office at 7am, and ducked as a dark object flew past his head. His shocked expression was met with an effusive apology.

"I am so, so sorry," Carla said. "When did you get in?"

Ben didn't answer, but walked out her office door.

"Come back," Carla called. "It's safe."

Ben walked back in with the dark object in his hand.

"Where did you find the ancient chalk board eraser, and why did I almost get canned with it? Were you an evil school teacher in a past life?"

Carla walked around her desk and took the eraser from her co-worker. "I found it in an antique store years ago. It is heavy enough for me to pitch across a room in frustration, but won't do any damage if my aim is off and it hits something."

"What were you aiming at?" Ben asked.

"Nothing," she replied. "It feels like we still have nothing."

"You're worried about your mom," Ben stated."

"Yes," she sighed, "and throwing this seemed better than punching something or flinging my coffee cup across the room. I also have a problem. I am suspicious of Will's girlfriend."

"Bella?"

"Doesn't it seem like something is off about her?"

"Like what?" Ben asked, as she sat behind her desk and he took one of the seats in front of it.

"She doesn't write!" Carla said.

"Okay," he said.

"That doesn't bother you?"

"A lot of people don't like to write," he said. "that's why recording devices were invented. People dictate and let someone else write their thoughts or correspondences."

"But those people do not move across the country and buy a condo to write a novel," she stated.

"I thought the novel was her grandmother's idea," he replied.

"Exactly!" Carla leaned forward in her seat. "Do you buy that story that the same grandmother sparing her from a violent death in some no-name, silver-mining pueblo in Mexico?"

"Wow," was all he said. "I think the town had a name."

"So what? Do you believe her?" Carla repeated.

"Obviously, you don't," he said.

"Remember the first time she was here and you told her about thallium? What if she poisoned my mother?"

"Bella? What reason would she have?" he asked.

"I don't know!" Carla was back out of her seat, and began to pace. "Maybe it was an experiment for the thriller she plans to write!"

"You just said she doesn't write," he calmly stated.

"I don't trust her," Carla said, stopping to look at Ben. "Her parents were murdered by the Mexican drug cartel because they had the wrong address?"

"It could happen," he said.

"She's from Colorado! Doesn't that send up a red flag?"

Carla stopped and looked at him. "You like her," she said. "Do you really believe she's as nice as she pretends to be?"

"I don't know her well, but I haven't had a reason to distrust her. Plus, I think Will really likes her. They spend a lot of time together and I believe him to be a rational, thoughtful guy. Don't you think if there were red flags he'd see them?"

"Will," Carla said.

"Yeah, Will," Ben repeated.

"No, he was just standing in the front hall. He heard what I said."

Carla dropped into her chair as they heard the front door to the office close. "Do you think he'll quit or just hate me?" she sighed.

"I think you need sleep," Ben said.

"I can't sleep," she stated. "You should see my mother. She can barely function."

"Thallium poisoning does a number on the body, but the effects can be temporary. She could have died, but she didn't. Focus on that."

When they heard the front door open again, Carla stood and hurried to the lobby.

"Oh, its you," she said, obviously disappointed.

"Hey, Ben," Mike said, looking past his distraught wife.

"She's had a bit of a meltdown," Ben said. "Good to see you."

Ben turned and disappeared into his lab, closing the door.

"Come here," Mike said, and opened his arms to Carla, who walked into them.

"I threw my eraser at Ben and accused Bella of poisoning my mother within earshot of Will," she cried. "And my mother isn't getting any better, and we still have too many loose ends."

"I passed Will leaving," was all Mike said. "Did we lose our lawyer?"

"Why are you so calm?" she asked, as she pushed away from him.

"I think I'll get a coffee," he said. "It just feels like one of us should be. By the way," he added as he headed to the conference room. "I got a text from Laurie on my way here. He said to call him as soon as I got in."

Mike got coffee and returned to Carla's office. She was sitting at her desk drinking coffee and waiting for him. He walked around her desk and leaned down to give her a kiss. "I believe things are going to break soon," he smiled. "Grandma Lettie said God told her they would."

"Where's my eraser?" she said, with a sheepish smile.

"Right here," he said, picking it up off her desk and handing it to her. "Need one more good throw?

"No," she said, "Maybe I just needed you. Put Laurie on speaker."

Mike did as told. Laurie answered on the first ring. "Mornin'!"

"Detective Baker," Mike said, "Hope you've got some good news for us. Carla's on speaker with me and she's really in need of some."

"Hey, Carla," he responded, "How's your mom doing?"

"It's been tough," Carla said.

"She's a fighter," Laurie encouraged.

"I hope so," was all Carla responded.

"Have you guys ever heard of Photo Phil?"

"Is that the ground hog that sees his shadow?" Mike asked.

"That's Punxsutawney Phil," Laurie said, "Not at all the same. Photo Phil is a little non-descript guy who lives on a trust fund and takes pictures."

"A photojournalist?" Carla asked.

"No. He doesn't show or create his pictures. He is only 5'3" tall with no distinguishing features. He slips in and out of places and just shoots pictures."

"Of what?" Mike asked.

"Whatever tickles his fancy," Laurie told them. "He might take a picture of a fly on someone's hat, or he might get caught taking pictures at a crime scene."

"So, the beach cops use him for … what?" Mike asked.

"It's not just at the beach. Police have spotted him all over the country. It's crazy. He's a quirky little guy, probably missing a few cars on his train, but on occasion he has given us a shot that has been helpful. We think he has a crush on one of our female officers. Early this morning she was sent a packet of pictures."

"With something of interest?"

"You could say that," Laurie said.

Carla and Mike both leaned forward; they could hear the smile in his voice.

"Photo Phil was just walking along Waccamaw avenue after a storm and saw a license plate that said 2BOOBS. He thought it was photo-worthy and wanted to see the hot babe that was driving the car. When it turned out to be a guy, he thought it was even funnier, so he shot a picture of him. He sent them to Officer Mia with the tag line—Gender Confusion."

"So, we have a picture of our killer?" Carla asked.

"We have more than that," Laurie said. "We know this guy. His name is Basil Stringer. He's ex-military. Our guys have talked to him at the firing range. He caught their attention because of his shooting precision. They said he's an ace with a short-nosed rifle."

"Does he have a record?" Mike asked.

"Never for anything this serious," Laurie told them. "But the word on the street is that he had been complaining about being in debt until a few months ago when he started buying rounds at the bar. He claimed if you had the talent, you could make a killing in less than an hour."

"So, he was a hired gun," Mike said.

"It seems that way," Laurie said, "Our guys are looking for him now. Like I said before, he has the ability to slip in and out of places without being noticed, but he's never been on our radar before."

"What's the plan when you pick him up?" Mike asked.

"We're going to have Mia ask to see his photo collection. If we're lucky, we might recognize others. If we're really lucky, we might see some of our big fish in compromising company."

"I meant this Basil guy," Carla explained.

"Oh, him." Laurie said. "He's toast. If Phil's photos give us anything, we might use him for a sting."

"Use String for a sting?" Mike said.

"Good one," Laurie chuckled.

"He's not going to be tried for murder?" Carla asked.

"Of course, he will be," Laurie said, "That's how we'll get what we want. South Carolina is a capital punishment state. If he wants to do time instead of choosing between a needle and the firing squad, Basil String will cooperate."

"What are you hoping to get from Photo Phil?" Mike asked.

"He's been doing this for years in several cities. If he lets Mia see his collection, it could take a while, but we might get lucky. Clark Creek and Marsha Barclay have both been at the beach on occasion. If our inconspicuous photographer happened to be in the right place at the right time, who knows?"

"A picture of Clark paying Basil would be nice," Carla said, "or one of someone breaking into my mother's house."

"Those might be a lot to ask for," he replied, "but we can hope for something useful. The pieces are falling into place, Carla. Give your mother my best."

Chapter 31

Marsha Barclay was in the company of her usual male companion in Bali when she received a text from Clark that read, unsavory project completed. Taking personal time. Will call when I get back.

"Bad news?" Budi asked, as he walked toward her, carrying two tall glasses of Aliya, a cocktail made with Ceylon Arrack, chilled coconut water, and a wedge of lime.

Taking the drink from him, she replied, "On the contrary, it is very good news. Tonight, we should celebrate with something stronger."

"I know what you like," he smiled.

"You always have," she replied, touching her glass to his.

Hours later Marsha received a text from Greg. This one contained a link to a US news report of a downed airplane that exploded on contact in a Texas field, seemingly headed to the Caribbean. The report said the bodies were burned beyond recognition, but that it appeared from flight documents to be a pilot, a stewardess, Dr. Martin Ashbury from Denver, Colorado, his wife Diana Ashbury, and his daughter Emma Ashbury.

The text from Greg read, who is taking the Doc's place?

Marsha was not surprised. Greg Walker was a man without a heart or soul. She smiled. He would prove to be very useful.

While Longstreet Campbell Investigations waited for calls from the LEO's concerning Basil String, Photo Phil's picture collection, and anything that might tie up some of their own loose ends, Carla called Roxie Winters.

"Did I interrupt anything?" Carla asked.

"I'm working on my resumé," Roxie said.

"Has your family been a help in job hunting?" Carla asked. "I remember when I was your age, I didn't want any help from family. Looking back, I'm not sure why."

"I haven't asked any of them," she said. "My one uncle is the mayor of the town I grew up in. My father has some VP job at Chesterton Corporation in Atlanta, and two of my uncles are attorneys," she said. "I'm sure I'll get lots of advice at the upcoming holiday get-togethers."

"It sounds like it," Carla tried to put a smile in her voice. "What was your major?"

"Paralegal," Roxie told her. "I'm applying to law firms in Savannah. I love living by the coast. I might even look into something in Charleston."

"Our attorney went to school and started his career in Charleston. Want me to ask if he could recommend the better firms?"

"Thanks," she said, "but I'd like to do this on my own—at least for now."

"Good for you," Carla said. "Can I ask you some questions about Taylor?"

"Sure," Roxie said.

"You said you didn't think she was dating anyone special, but where did she go to meet guys? Did she hang out at college bars or put her profile online? If I wanted to figure out when she went off grid, where should I start looking?"

"Taylor really didn't do either of those things," Roxie said. "She was a little older than some of us and she thought typical college boys were immature."

Carla waited as Roxie seemed to be considering her answer. "Taylor loved Savannah as much as I do," she said. "There were a couple restaurants and sports bar where we would go together. I think sometimes she went to the city alone. We hung out a lot, but we never lived together."

"Can you give me a list of those places?" Carla asked. "Maybe I'll check them out and see if anyone remembers her being with one guy in particular. My husband and I have been talking about making a trip to Savannah. We could combine work and pleasure."

"Let me know what weekend you pick," Roxie said. "I'd love to meet you in person. My life is a bit slow now that classes are over and I haven't started a job yet."

"I have a feeling it won't take long for some lucky company or firm to snatch you up," Carla told her. "I'll talk to my husband and text you our plans. I'd love to meet you in person also. Don't forget to send me that list of places Taylor frequented."

"I'll do it as soon as we get off this call," Roxie said.

"Good luck job hunting," Carla told her.

As Carla's call ended, Mike walked into her office. "Want to leave early?" he asked.

"Is something up?" she wanted to know.

"I'm tired and I'm guessing you are, too," he said. "Let's stop by Taproom, have a glass of wine, relax a little and maybe get to bed early."

"I should go by my mother's," Carla said.

"I just got off the phone with Longstreet," Mike said. "He's taking her to the mountains. They already left."

"What?" she said alarmed. "Without even checking with me? I don't appreciate him taking over."

"Carla," Mike said. "According to him, it was your mother's idea. I don't think he was comfortable taking her alone, so Mac and Dolley are going with them."

"He still should have contacted me," she said.

"He just called from a gas stop somewhere in North Carolina. He said your mother didn't want him to call you, because she said you needed a break. Her exact words were that last night you looked terrible."

Carla's mouth dropped open.

"He did make her talk to her doctor before he agreed to take her, and he insisted Mac and Dolley had to accompany them. Let her have this time. I'm sure her limitations are more upsetting to her than they even are to you. She's trying to be positive. Give them a few days away from the problems here."

Carla sighed a deep sigh. "Okay," she said, "you might be right."

As she closed her laptop, her phone notified her she had a new text. It was the list from Roxie. They both stuck their heads in their associates' offices to say they were leaving early. The responses were waves and smiles.

Once in the car, Carla opened the text.

"Anything important?" Mike asked.

"It's a list of bars and restaurants in Savannah that Roxie and Taylor used to frequent. How about we take a few days off and go to Savannah. If I'm in a hotel and know my mother is in the mountains, I might be able to sleep. I feel like I could sleep for days if I could just completely relax."

"I promise to do my best to help in that arena," Mike looked at her and smiled.

"That's a suspicious grin," she said.

"I was thinking of ways to help you forget your troubles and relax."

"Umph." Carla pretended to be considering his offer. Then, she smiled and said, "lets go home and order a pizza."

"Why?"

"My mother is away, and I think I'd like to see how you think you can help me relax."

"I don't think, Kid," he smiled. "I know!"

Carla laughed. She could feel herself relaxing already.

The next day, Carla and Mike left for Savannah. They stopped in Charleston, South Carolina for lunch and walked around the market. Mike picked out a pair of earrings he liked for Carla. She thought the gesture was sweet. It was less than two hours from Charleston to Savannah. Mike had called the Bellwether House, a charming place located downtown. The only room they had available was a king with a spa bath. Carla thought it was a bit excessive. "Humor me," had been Mike's response. They weren't meeting Roxie until the next day, so they had a nice dinner with wine before going back to their room. Carla had no trouble sleeping.

Roxie was nothing like Carla had imagined. She had expected a petite girl with a pixie face. Roxanne Winters was tall and slender with chiseled cheekbones, and a sophisticated appearance. They talked for a while in the lobby of the Bellwether to make a game plan. Roxie gave them the order that made sense to her. She knew the times that each place was usually busy. The first place they went to was because it had the best and most reasonable lunch menu. They stopped at one more restaurant just to show Taylor's picture to the hostess and bartender. Everyone seemed to remember Roxie; many remembered Taylor as the girl who often came with her.

No one was hungry for a meal in the evening, and Roxie's last stop was a sports bar that she said was a favorite of hers and Taylor. They sat at the bar and placed orders for Spinach Dip and Homemade Pretzels, along with three beers. The bartender was glad to see Roxie, and said of course he remembered Taylor. The chatted like old friends. Carla excused herself to use the restroom which was located in a back hallway with walls covered with photos of patrons. When she came out of the restroom, she stopped to look at the wall of pictures. She decided it made her feel old seeing so many young faces enjoying a night at the bar. Suddenly, she recognized Taylor in a picture with a guy. She quickly went to the bar to get Mike and Roxie.

Pointing to the picture, she said, "Do you recognize the guy Taylor is with?"

Roxie looked at the picture and laughed, "Sure," she said.

"Could that be a boyfriend she would leave town with and not tell anyone?" Mike asked, exchanging looks with Carla.

"No," Roxie said. "He wasn't a boyfriend. That's Marty. He's a business associate of my fathers."

"She looks awfully cozy with him in that picture," Carla said.

"That's just the way Marty is," Roxie said. "He doesn't even live around here. He's only in town a few times a year."

"If she did hook up with him," Carla asked, "would she maybe be embarrassed to tell you because he was older and a friend of your fathers?"

"I don't know," Roxie said. "That would be a big deal to drop out of school and move to Colorado to be with him. I don't know how trustworthy he was."

"Why do you say that?" Mike asked her.

"I mean he always seemed nice when we met him here," she began.

"Always?" Mike asked. "I thought you said he was only here a few times a year."

"Last spring he was here every couple weeks but I haven't seen him since."

"Why didn't you think he was trustworthy?" Carla asked.

"It was something my father once said about him," Roxie said, thinking as she spoke. "I don't remember exactly what his comment was, but it surprised me because Marty always was nice when he was around Taylor and me."

Carla took a picture of the picture and they went back to the bar. When they finished their beers, Carla said she'd had enough of bars for one day. They dropped Roxie off at her car, thanked her for the tour, and said they'd keep in touch. Neither of them spoke immediately as they drove the half block to the Bellwether.

When Mike turned off the engine, Carla said, "Well, does that tie up loose ends or just create new threads?"

"I'm not sure," Mike said, "but we know where to look for Taylor. Who could have known our cases would tie together this way."

The face in the picture that Roxie identified as Marty was the person known to Carla and Mike as Clark Creek.

Chapter 32

Sandy, Dolley and Mac were enjoying their stay in the mountains. Carla talked to her mother and Dolley every day. Her mother sounded happy. Carla sensed an improvement in her speech.

"She is improving, isn't she?" Carla asked Dolley who called her back from the downstairs living room.

"Her speech is almost back to normal," Dolley said. "It's good to see her smiling again. I think her memory is coming back, and she is able to think and concentrate a little better. Mac has been giving us Bible lessons in an effort to improve her concentration and memory."

"I almost lost her," Carla said.

"But you didn't," Dolley reminded her. "She was covered in prayer, and it seems God still has a purpose for her here. Between you and me, I'm wondering if part of that purpose involves Longstreet."

"What do you mean?"

"He's different with her. Mac says she is softening him like I softened Mac. I wouldn't go that far," Dolley chuckled, "but it is cute the way he helps her with little things."

"But she's improving," Carla stated.

"Yes, dear, she is improving—a little bit every day. I think the plan is to come back the end of the week. You'll be able to see for yourself. However, it is beautiful up here."

Carla hung up the phone, reassured, but still anxious to see her mother for herself. She had researched thallium poisoning and knew the odds of Sandy living through direct exposure had been slim. If it hadn't been for Ben's quick recognition of the situation, and the hospital's early administration of the Prussian Blue, she probably would have died. Ben claimed the coma might have helped because it probably slowed the absorption by her organs, of course, he said that was just a guess. There was not a lot of information on thallium poisoning. It was usually only seen in slow, time-release exposure unrealized until symptoms are difficult to reverse.

In his desire to avoid the death penalty, Basil String had admitted to breaking into Sandy's house and infusing the poison into her new tube of toothpaste. He had been given specific instructions on how to do it by a video call from some guy named Greg. He said Greg referred to some woman named Marsha, but he didn't know who that was.

For that reason, the Myrtle Beach police had kept String's arrest very restricted to a need to know few. String knew he was in big trouble and was smart enough to cooperate, knowing those who had instructed him and paid him would never admit to even knowing him. He also identified Clark Creek from a picture, saying he didn't know the guy's name, but he had been introduced to him more than a year ago by a dealer named Matt who had died of an overdose at the airport. Clark Creek's criminal activity was becoming more and more obvious. An APB had been put out on him across state lines.

"What do you mean they are letting him go," Carla shouted. "Basil String killed Justin Shoemaker and poisoned my mother. If they let him go, I'll find him and kill him myself!" she declared.

Mike closed her office door and said, "Settle down and listen. He isn't free; he is being released as a mole. He's going to lead us to Clark Creek and Marsha Barclay."

"We don't need him," Carla said, pacing her office. "We have enough on Clark. We already know he's connected to Marsha and now we have testimony concerning this Greg guy. What if String loses the detail following him? The police have lost supposed witnesses before. You know they have."

"We won't lose this one," Mike assured her. "The Feds want these guys, too."

"For illegal trafficking of all kinds," Carla said. "I know that, Mike, but I want him for killing Justin and nearly killing my mother. We have to do something to insure he doesn't slip his tail and disappear."

"We are," he told her, "He has a second tail."

"Who?"

Mike smiled. "Rambo will not lose an amateur like Basil String."

"Oh," Carla said, slowing her pace and sitting at her desk. "Okay, that makes me more confident. So, what's their strategy?"

"Laurie said String has a way to get back to this Greg guy. He leaves a message on what appears to be a burner phone, and the guy is supposed to get back to him. He tells the guy he got picked up on suspicion, but the cops didn't have enough to hold him. He demands a large sum of money and a phony passport so he can leave the country. He threatens to tell the police about Greg and Clark, and that Clark mentioned some woman named Marsha."

"Do you think this Greg will buy his story? They're not going to give a guy like String what he's asking for," Carla reasoned.

"Laurie said when they presented their plan, he could see String running the scenario through his head. He probably believes he can ditch the police and do exactly as he is threatening. He thinks he's going to get rich and disappear. The guy isn't very smart."

"But will Clark and Marsha fall for his story?" she asked.

"It doesn't matter," Mike said, "the odds are they will send someone to eliminate poor String, but before that happens, we'll have one more link to our two masterminds—a direct link and hopefully a location to take them out. The Feds will be on every communication in real time."

"And Rambo won't lose him," Carla stated.

"No," Mike assured her, "he won't. The other good thing is that Longstreet has your mother and Dolley far from all of this."

"Dolley?"

"She was abducted once by people connected in to these criminals. Marsha and Clark may not know they are at the end of their ropes, but they still have long memories. Now that Myrtle Beach is interested, anyone who can connect the dots to them is at risk. I wouldn't want to be this Greg guy right now. My guess is that he's probably dispensable, too."

"Do you think Taylor's in danger?" Carla asked.

"I don't know," he answered. "She sure didn't pick a good guy to take off with. Even if she doesn't know about his criminal side, she could just find herself with the wrong people at a bad time."

"I'm worried about her," Carla said.

"All we can do is pray for her," Mike told her.

"When I was looking into her background to find someone who might know where she was, there was nothing," Carla said.

"I know," Mike replied. "I think she is probably in over her head."

"No," Carla repeated, "There was no one. She doesn't have a background. It was weird."

"Well," Mike said. "If we find Clark, we may find her. Hopefully, she'll just be disappointed and not worse."

Both Rob and the police tailing String watched him climb out his back window with a backpack, and go to an off-site banking terminal to withdraw whatever he had in the bank. He then hid the backpack under a fallen tree in an area near SC-707 behind his complex before going back, through the window and walking out his front door. He nodded to the cops he knew were watching him.

String had his own plan to out-maneuver this Greg guy. As soon as he had the big payout and a new passport, he'd ditch the police and be gone. No one would ever know where he was. He wasn't going to leave the good ole USA. He had a buddy living in northern Minnesota. He'd use the name on his new and unknown to the police passport and make a new life in the land of cold winters and 1,000 lakes.

When Greg got the call from String, he contacted Marsha who was not happy to hear from him.

"I'm not in the country," she said. "What do you expect me to do about this guy. Eliminate the threat. I'm tired of amateurs. If you expect to impress me that you are able to be my number two, then do the job yourself."

"Number two?" he smiled. "What about Clark?"

"He's dead," she said, "You are the one that told me."

"I never met Clark," Greg said, "I only knew Marty."

"Marty was Clark, you fool," Marsha told him. "I'm coming home in a few days. I expect you to do as you're told. I'm counting on you."

Greg knew this was his big chance. Marsha Barclay was not only confiding in him, but she was counting on him. He wouldn't let her down. He sat back in his chair and let it all sink in. Clark and Marty were one and the same. That was a big revelation. He wondered why that had been necessary, but he figured with time he would understand more. Greg had money, but not compared to what he had observed with Marty. Now he was to become the new Marty, only he was smart enough not to let Marty's fate happen to him. He'd never piss off Marsha and he'd never fall in love. You had to know how to use women without letting them control you. Marsha Barclay, he smiled, you've met your match.

Greg got back to Basil String, agreeing with his terms. He said he was sending a woman to deliver the money and the passport in person. He said it would take a few days, and then he set up a time and place for the transaction. Greg asked String if he was being followed by the police. String said if he was, not to worry. He knew how to lose them. He'd done it before.

Greg decided to pull out an old license in the name of Bill Jones that he hadn't used in years. On the day before he was to meet Basil String, he flew to Greensboro, North Carolina, rented a car, and drove to the beach. At the Myrtle Beach Visitor Center on Highway 501, he went into the ladies' room after midnight and came out dressed in perfect drag. His slight build helped his disguise. The billowy sleeves on the blouse he wore shielded his muscular biceps. The loose-fitting slacks and the long, blonde wig would be easy to lose in the location he had chosen. He would walk away in tourist's shorts, tee shirt and flip flops, get on a bike and be gone before what he had done was discovered.

Basil String was anxious for this meet to be over. He had a plan that worked well for him. He was supposed to meet the woman Greg was sending, behind the Scotchman Store near the intersection of Bypass-17 and Harbor Towne Drive. He knew this area. He kept a motorcycle hidden at an abandoned trailer only blocks from there. He would let the cops see him going to the dark side of the store, away from the lights of the gas pumps. He would get what was his from this woman and then he would take off on foot. He was smart and fast. Before the cops realize he was missing, he'd be at his bike and gone.

String knew the cops would apprehend the woman he was meeting when she walked back to her car at the gas pump, but she wouldn't know where String went. She could, however, lead them to the real criminals, which was what they ultimately wanted. String was done living on the wrong side of the law. With his newly acquired fortune, he could live in a remote land of winter snow and summer beauty. It sounded good to him.

The sting didn't go well for Basil String. The woman didn't hand String an envelope. She plunged a knife into his heart and let his lifeless body drop to the ground. She quietly walked to the ladies' room on the side of the building and lost her disguise. Leaving the restroom, Greg quickly walked without his wig and women's attire to a Harley he had positioned earlier in the day not far from the restroom. In his beach clothes, he jump-started the bike and drove off as the cops were positioned to apprehend both of their targeted criminals.

Greg took Port Drive the short distance to SC-707 where he could quickly access US-17 from which he could get back to Greensboro and home. What Greg didn't realize was that the rider on the black bike that followed him up the entrance ramp to US-17 was no ordinary rider. US-17 would eventually become State Road 9, which would lead to I-74. Greg had taken this road before. He rode along, enjoying the South Carolina sunset. He was traveling west toward a lucrative future back in the western mountains that he loved. Maybe there would be a way to purchase Marty's log house. The idea it might one day be his had never entered his mind, but he would dream bigger dreams from now on.

Greg heard the bike approaching, and glanced in his mirror. He had noticed a similar bike and rider when he originally merged onto the highway. His heart rate increased as it got closer. As the two bikes crossed the Waccamaw River before reaching the town of Longs, the rider on the black bike pulled next to Greg with a gun pointed at him. Greg hit the accelerator as the other biker forced him into the guard railing of the bridge. Greg's leg was slammed between the bridge and his cycle. The pain and fear caused him to let go of his bike, tumbling his body over the railing and into the river. The other rider slowed and pulled off onto the riverbank. He waited until the body surfaced, floating face down. He then returned to the highway. It didn't have to end that way, but his job was done.

Marsha Barclay was picked up that same night at LaGuardia as she entered the country. They had more than enough to put her away, no matter how high-priced her legal team might be. When asked about Marty Ashbury, she said she heard he died in a plane crash. They told her his ID's were found at the crash site, but they had not officially identified the body as Dr. Ashbury. She merely asked them who else it could have been, because she claimed she had no idea.

Even hearing that, the people at Longstreet Campbell Investigations believed their loose ends were being tied together.

Chapter 33

Dolley and Mac were throwing a party to celebrate Sandy's newest lab report that showed the thallium was finally out of her body, and the fact that the bad guys were all either dead or in prison. There was no longer any danger in the paradise known as Murrells Inlet, South Carolina.

Carla, Mike and Will texted that they would be late. Will had a meeting with Adam to which Carla and Mike asked to be a part. Will and Adam sat in the conference room with coffee just having casual conversation.

"So, do you like this woman?" Adam asked with a smile.

"I really do," Will said, as Carla and Mike entered.

They greeted him and got coffee before sitting at the table.

"That's great," Adam said, continuing the interrupted chat. "I'm a big fan of solid, long-term relationships. I know the old joke is that married men don't live longer—it just seems that way, but I think it's true."

"The joke?" Mike laughed.

"No," Adam said, "They live longer because they are happier. A good marriage benefits the mental health of both parties."

"Is this like a men's therapy session?" Carla asked.

"No," Adam smiled. "Will was just telling me he's in love."

When Carla raised an eyebrow, Will said, "I never said love."

"You didn't have to, friend," Adam smiled.

"Speaking of parties, we have one to get to, so let's move on to business."

Mike proceeded to tell Adam a little about the criminal activity they had been investigating that originated with contraband of various kinds being hidden within legitimate shipping orders."

He picked up a picture as they were interrupted.

"Did you start without me?" Laurie asked, as he entered the room.

"I thought you'd be at the party," Carla said.

"The same party you're supposed to be at?" he asked, extending his hand to Adam Chesterton. "I'm Detective Baker of the Myrtle Beach Police Force. My condolences on your father's death. I understand you took over his position at the company."

Adam looked from Carla to Mike, as Laurie took a seat.

"Am I in some sort of trouble?" Adam asked.

"No," Laurie told him. "I believe Mike was about to show you a picture. I'd like to know if this man looks familiar to you."

"No," Adam said. "I don't think I know him."

"How about in this picture?" Mike asked, showing him a picture of the same guy exiting his company with Duncan Winters.

"Duncan knows this guy," Adam stated. "Who is he?"

"He was a big player in an illegal, international shipping ring that was recently broken up."

"Oh my God!" Adam exclaimed. "Does this mean Duncan is mixed up with him?"

"We don't know, but if he is, we aren't sure if he is shipping through your company or if they had another arrangement. We have no reason other than Duncan Winters to suspect Chesterton of any wrong doing. How well do you know him?"

"His father was my father's driver for decades. Duncan and I first met as young boys."

"You know his father is the Mayor of Harpton," Laurie stated.

"Of course," Adam said, "and I know there have been allegations of wrong doing in his office, but since he was never arrested or convicted, I chose to believe they were just political gossip."

"The Georgia Bureau has been watching them closely," Laurie said. "Before anything goes down, it would be wise for you to have an extensive external audit of your accounting, shipping and personnel."

"I will," he said, looking very concerned. "Do you really think Duncan is crooked?"

"We do," Laurie said, "but it may not involve Chesterton Inc."

"I certainly hope not," he said, glancing down at the other picture on the table. "Let me look at that picture."

Mike handed him the picture of Taylor and Marty.

"Is this the same guy?" Adam asks, "He looks different."

"The guy has different looks through the years and goes by different names. Does he look familiar in this picture?"

"No," Adam said. "I still don't recognize the guy, but the girl looks like a girl I picked up hitching at a truck stop years ago.

"You know Taylor Reese?" Carla asked, leaning forward.

"I only met her one night at a truck stop. She wanted a ride to Myrtle Beach and that's where I was headed. We drove through the night," he said, not mentioning that they spent part of it in the back of his cab. "Her name wasn't Taylor, though" he added. "Her name was Sally."

Since everyone had a party to attend, Adam thanked them for giving him a heads up, and left.

The three at the table were silent when Will walked back into the room.

"You believe him, don't you?" he asked.

"He seemed sincere in everything he said. We have no reason to doubt him at this point. I'd like you to contact him at some point and request the results from his audit," Laurie said.

"I already suggested that as he left. Do they know for sure that guy is dead?" he asked, pointing to the pictures.

"The FBI believes he is," Laurie said, as he left. "Gotta go."

"We could talk about this stuff all afternoon," Carla said, standing. "Let's go to a party. It seems you have a love waiting for you there."

"Give me a break," Will said. "I didn't say love—he did."

"But you didn't contradict him," Carla challenged.

"No, I didn't," he smiled, "but I'm not telling you before I tell her."

"Well," Carla patted his chest as she passed him. "Don't take too long. There's a time limit on how long I can keep a secret."

The party was in full force when Will walked into Dolley's home, decorated with balloons and happy people. Bella walked up to him and started to speak, when he pulled her into a hug and covered her mouth with his in a full-blown kiss.

"Whoa!" was the word heard around the room.

"Will," Bella laughed when she came up for air. "What was that about?"

"Can't a guy kiss his girl in front of his friends?"

They walked into the room arm-in-arm, as Dolley winked at Bella, and Mac bumped Will's shoulder, saying, "Good for you."

There was a muted football game on the big-screen TV, however, the play-by-play calls could be heard on the smaller TV in the den where Mac was headed with three beers that Tap, Chip, and Longstreet were waiting for.

Barb and Sandy were talking at the kitchen table with Rose and Elsa, who had Daisy and Astrid on their laps. Devon was in the den with the guys. Barb had taken Jake to court and had been granted full custody of Josh and Mandy. He had finally crossed a line that even Barb couldn't forgive. The kids were with Jake's parents today who had moved to the beach to help with childcare. They also were finally convinced that until Jake was ready to change, nothing anyone else said or did would matter. Rumor had it he was living in Florida with his latest employed girlfriend.

"Dolley," Reba called, "I think these mushrooms are ready to come out of the oven."

"Do you need help?" Rose beckoned from the table.

"We've got it," Dolley responded, and then asked Reba, "Do you know when you're leaving yet?"

"My rent is paid until the end of December," she replied. "I'm so excited, Dolley, to be given the opportunity to write this next memoir."

"You'll be in Washington?" Dolley asked.

"Bellingham," she responded, "just south of Canada on a bay. I've never been in the northwest part of our country."

"Neither have I," Dolley said. "It sounds cold."

"It doesn't get much colder than here," Reba said, "but of course the summers don't get near as hot. You'll have to look it up on a map. It looks like a pretty cool place. Of course, my main job will be documenting my employer's story and researching the area."

"Are you nervous to go so far away from home?" Dolley asked.

"I'm actually excited," she said. "I came here alone and made friends. I believe I can do it again."

"I believe you can too," Dolley said. "I will continue to pray for you."

"I will never forget you, Dolley," Reba said. "I don't know that I will ever accept that God is as personal as you say he is."

"Look how he's taken care of you," Dolley said.

"Maybe I've taken care of myself," Reba replied. "I had parents that preached at me my whole life, but they seemed more interested in pleasing God than loving me. It made an impression."

"You have friends here who love you for who you are and believe God is directing your life," Dolley said. "I am counting on you understanding that one day soon."

Reba gave Dolley a hug. "And that's why I'll never forget you," she said.

"Keep me updated on your journey," Dolley said. "Mac and I do care about you."

"I know," Reba said. "I will."

"It's about time," Will shouted as Carla and Mike walked into the room, carrying a bottle of wine. "Where's Laurie? I thought he was coming,"

"He left right after you," Carla said. "Maybe he had to pick up Marti."

"She lives ten minutes from here," Will said.

"What can I tell you," Carla responded before walking over to kiss her mother.

"The food is all ready," Dolley called across the room. "Will, can you corral the guys in from the den?"

"Sure," he said.

The guys came in and all were quiet as Mac gave a short blessing over the food. As everyone said, "amen," Laurie and Marti walked in holding hands.

"What took you so long?" Will asked. "She doesn't live that far away."

"I had to stop at the jewelers," Laurie said, lifting Marti's hand into the air. "I misjudged the size last weekend."

The food no longer held everyone's interest. Everyone crowded around Laurie and Marti to offer congratulations and see her diamond ring.

Mac walked to the kitchen island and put his arm around Dolley's shoulders. "Our kids are doing okay, aren't they?" he smiled.

"Yes," she replied, tearfully. "And Sandy is right in the middle of everyone as though nothing happened. God is so good."

"She still has a ways to go," Mac said.

"I know," Dolley answered, as Sandy looked a little wobbly, and Longstreet put his arm around her shoulders, "but she won't be recovering alone."

"No," he smiled, "She won't."

The party wasn't as long or as boisterous as parties in the past. Longstreet took Sandy home when she looked tired. Tap and Elsa, Chip and Rose left early with their little kids.

Eventually, it was just Carla and Mike, who were helping to clean up.

"I'm happy for Laurie and Marti," Carla said.

"It looks like Will and Bella might not be far behind," Dolley said.

"I'm happy for them too," she said.

"What happened to that internal gut thing?" Mike teased.

When Dolley gave a questioning look, Carla said, "I didn't warm up to Bella right away, but I was wrong. She's different from anyone I have ever known, but that's the great thing about our God, we all don't have to be the same."

"He's the God of diversity," Mac said, "We're all different and that's okay."

Chapter 34

Three months later, Mark Martin and his wife Diana, woke to the sun rising over the three-bedroom villa he had purchased in the Dominican Republic. Ten-year-old Emma slept in the room next to them.,

Lying next to her husband Diana asked, "She was yours all along, wasn't she?"

"Yeah," he said.

"Why doesn't she know that?"

"I told you I wasn't a good man until I met you," he said.

"I don't believe that," Diana told him.

"Nevertheless," he said, "It's true."

"Well, I'm glad those days are over," she said, moving closer to him and putting her head on his shoulder.

"Diana," he said, seriously, "If something ever happens to me, there is a steal box buried near the avocado tree behind the house. In it are all the papers you would need to keep the house and to keep Emma. My will and all my financial papers are there, too. The lawyer who helped with the sale of the house has copies of everything. I trust him and you can too."

"Don't talk about stuff like that," Diana said. "You know I don't care about your money."

"I know. But if you need help, go to him. I want you to be happy here, Diana. You have Emma whether I have a long life with you or not. I am older than you, remember," he smiled.

Diana leaned up and kissed his cheek. "You only look older when you need a shave and these gray whiskers show." Patting his still muscular chest, she added, "You have the body and mind of a much younger man. I don't want to hear any more talk about you getting old and dying. I won't let you!"

It was still early, and wasn't long before Diana heard Marty's deep, even breathing. As she lay at his side, she knew a contentment she remembered she had first felt in the cab of a semi.

"God," she whispered, "Thank you for blessing the unorthodox path my life has taken. I was born Karen. My mother was always high and my father indifferent or mean. I ran away to survive and became Sally. As Sally I lived with whoever would take me in, worked multiple jobs, some I'm not proud of, and saved nearly every penny I made. I met a girl who knew a guy that could get me legitimate-looking creds, so I became Taylor. As Taylor, I met a group of people who knew you and cared about me. I got an education, but still wasn't sure I could trust you as they did. I think I couldn't understand love, so I still couldn't understand you.

"Then I met Marty. I sensed his past hadn't been any better than mine. For some reason he loved me, and as he protected me, I watched him change; and I began to change, too. I began to feel loveable, and then you sent me Emma, who needed my love. I could relate to this sweet, needy little girl, and I wanted to protect her. So, here we are. I am ready to be yours, God. If Marty, someday, is no longer around, I believe you have given Emma and I a life we can handle, with your help, of course. Thank you, God. Amen."

Diana sighed and fell asleep tucked under both her husband and her heavenly Father's strong, protective arms.

Later that morning, the happy family walked through the outdoor market after enjoying a leisurely breakfast. As Diana and Emma were examining some fabrics, Mark entered a small shop he had frequented before. The owner often had received shipments of high-quality cigars for which he knew Mark would pay top-dollar. As the owner walked into the back room, a tall man wearing a turban and sporting a dark beard, walked in behind him. Mark turned and smiled. The man merely nodded, and closed the door.

The hair on Mark's arms alerted him to danger. He called to the owner that he'd come back for the cigars later, and attempted to walk around the dark-skinned stranger. After he passed him, the man's arm quickly came around Mark's neck and in one swift motion, snapped his neck before quietly laying his breathless body on the ground. Budi silently exited the shop, closed the door, and walked away. Slipping through the crowd into an alley, he discarded the turban and the beard. At the far end of the alley, he heralded a taxi to the airport and flew back to Bali. He knew he would never see Marsha again. This had been the one last thing he could do for her.

Allen Longstreet sat with Sandy on the screened-in back porch of his mountain home watching the sky turn pink, orange, yellow and red as the sun set. Two big dogs sat at their feet.

"There's nothing like a sunset," Sandy sighed. "This one tonight is especially beautiful."

"Do you like them better in the mountains or at the ocean?" he asked.

"I like them best wherever we are together," she smiled at him.

Allen reached over and took her hand, playing with the shiny new ring he loved seeing on her finger. "Do you think they'll be unhappy we didn't invite them to our wedding?" he asked.

"Probably at first," she said.

"Are you sorry we didn't?"

"No," she smiled at him. "This time it felt too special to share."

"You don't think Carla will be upset?"

"I think she was a little upset when she thought we were moving here to live together without being married," Sandy laughed.

"She and Mike lived together," he reminded her.

"Yes," Sandy said, "but I'm her mother. Maybe she didn't care, but I think she did."

"When are they coming this way?" he asked.

"I talked to Carla this afternoon. She and Dolley are trying to put together a time the four of them can drive up together. Dolley doesn't want Mac driving this far himself."

"I hope she didn't tell him that," Allen laughed.

"Carla said it would be within the next two weeks."

"It's like they've always been a part of my life," he commented.

"I remember when it didn't feel that way to me. They were part of your life, but I felt very left out," she said.

"When would that have been?" he asked.

"That night you all got dressed up and went to a dinner dance in DC. I was so jealous of Melissa. It felt like she was part of an inner circle that was supposed to include me, not her."

Allen again rubbed his thumb back and forth over her ring. "There was never any reason for you to have been jealous of Melissa," he said.

"Even during those years when you and she lived up here alone?" Sandy asked.

"You mean the years you were married to Drake?" he responded.

"We were married," she said.

"I'm very aware of that," he replied.

"You chose Ike over me," she told him.

"Not likely," he laughed, then added, "Seriously, I was a fool back then, but not anymore. Everything before now is the past, and I'm grateful for parts of it, but I'm more interested in our future."

"Me, too," she said, "but there really wasn't anything between you and Melissa? I know I shouldn't ask because I was married, but I'm asking."

"We were partners and we were good friends through the years, but we were never lovers," he said.

They sat a minute without speaking as the sky became dark.

"It's getting cooler out here," Sandy said, as the wind became stronger. "I'm not sure this blanket is enough."

Suddenly the roof was being pelted by large drops of rain.

"Let's go in," Allen said, "I'll build a fire."

"Okay, she smiled, "but can we leave the doors to the porch open for a while?"

"With the fire going?" he asked. "I thought you were getting cold."

"But I love a rainy night," she said.

He smiled at her, "So do I."

Allen reached for her hand to help her up, and then took her blanket as they walked inside.

Once inside the great room, he turned on a small lamp, tucked the blanket around her, and walked to the massive fireplace to start the fire.

"I'm so glad all the danger in our lives is over," Sandy said.

"I think everyone is," he replied.

"Do you remember when I first met Marsha Barclay? She came up to the table at Dead Dog Saloon and started asking me questions. Dolley told her I was hard of hearing," Sandy laughed.

As the kindling took and the fire started to blaze, Allen said, "I remember when Carla and Mike and I first told you and Dolley about the Fuentes brothers and the two of you announced you didn't need anyone to protect you because you both had guns. You wanted to buy a purse with a built-in gun pocket."

"You thought we were crazy," she smiled.

"Everyone thought you were crazy," he said.

"It was right after Marsha showed up that you took me to get my new car. Remember that? We had breakfast together."

"We have a lot of happy memories of the beach," he said, coming to sit next to her.

"A few sad ones, too," she said.

"Are you thinking of Patsy?"

"How did you know?" she asked.

"I know you," he whispered, as she leaned her head on his shoulder.

"There is one thing I'd change about our wedding," he said, after a few minutes of silently watching the fire.

"What?" she asked. "I thought it was perfect."

Allen pulled his phone from his pocket and after a couple taps, he set it on the coffee table and stood as Eddie Rabbit started to sing.

"May I have this dance, Mrs. Longstreet," he said, holding out his hand to her.

Sandy stood and he led her to the space in front of the fireplace.

"We didn't get to dance when we got married," Allen said.

"You do realize there are more romantic songs than 'I love a Rainy Night' don't you?"

"Not for me," he said, as they swayed together in the firelight with the rain hitting the porch roof. "That night I carried you home from my house, you were crying over Billy and I remember wondering what it would feel like if you were to love me like that."

"You didn't think that," she challenged, looking up at him.

"I swear to God I did," he said.

"You never told me," she replied.

"It never seemed appropriate before now," he smiled. "Loving you and having your love … well, I hope we have decades to dance in the rain together. 'I love a Rainy Night' will always be a romantic song for me. If I wasn't afraid we'd fall down the mountain in the dark, I'd drag you outside to dance in the rain."

Sandy laughed. "We're going to make great memories of our own, Allen, and I don't think anything could be more romantic than listening to the rain and dancing before a fire with you as my husband. Next time we're at the beach and it rains, it would be fun to go out and dance on the beach in the rain. Do you think we could do that?"

"I promise we can," he said, and heard her sigh as they danced while he softly sang in her ear, "Oh, how I love a rainy night. It makes me feel high. Yes, I love a rainy night. And I love you too. Oh, I love you too."

When they finished dancing, Hero barked as an empty plastic glass blew off a table. The wind was stronger and it was raining much harder.

Allen walked over to close the double doors. "It looks like we're in for a storm," he said.

"I don't mind storms outside when it's warm and cozy in here," Sandy said.

"You've have weathered all kinds of storms in life," he said as they sat together facing the fire again. "You have always impressed me with your positive spirit, no matter what trials came your way."

"It's not my spirit," she said. "It's God's spirit in me. I was almost ready to give up this year. Don't you remember how I failed to believe things were going to get better?"

"You got discouraged, but you didn't fail to believe. Once again, you looked to your heavenly Father and you didn't give up."

"I am so honored to be your wife, Allen," she said, taking his hand.

Allen laughed. "I am the honored one. There is nothing in this world that inspires me as you do."

"Your life has not been easy either," she said. "I'm sure there have been many times you should have died, but God saved you for me; us for each other. Every life has storms, Allen, but we have survived ours. I'm glad we're looking to a future together."

"Always positive," he smiled, giving her shoulders a squeeze. "May all our storms be behind us."

"But if they aren't," she said, "We need to promise to never lose hope."

As they smiled at each other, Allen said simply, "Together, we'll never lose hope, no matter the storm."

The fire crackled, the rain hit the roof, and Sandy and Allen were content. They knew they were exactly where they were meant to be.

Three things will last
forever

faith, hope, and love

and the greatest of
these

is love.

1 Corinthians 13:13

Murrells Inlet Beach Series

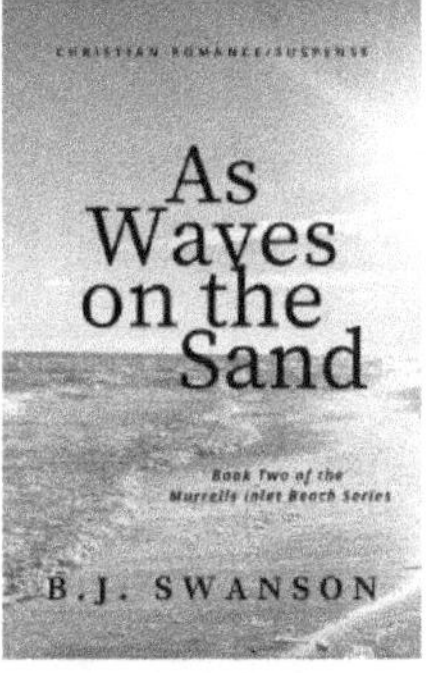

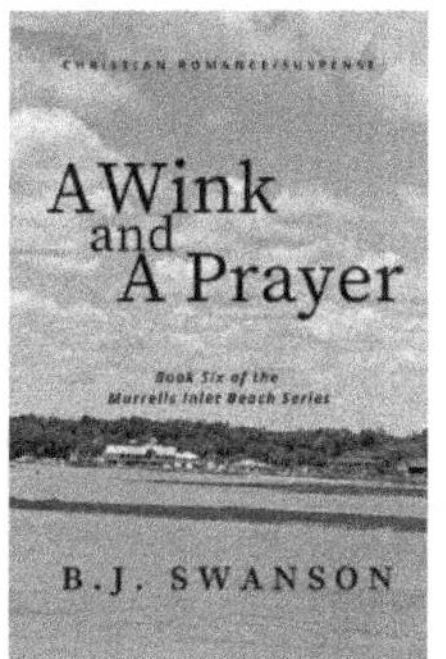

Watch for new series

All available on Amazon.com

www.ingramcontent.com/pod-product-compliance
Lightning Source LLC
Chambersburg PA
CBHW070746160726
48004CB00001B/67